PATIENCE COUNTY WAR

SOREN PAUL PETREK

1/12

ISBN: 1467931314
ISBN 13: 9781467931311

For my sons,
Max and Riley

INTRODUCTION

Two detectives watched from an unmarked patrol car as a man entered a dilapidated warehouse. The driver's muscular body strained the fabric of his rumpled suit, while his older partner reclined comfortably in the passenger seat, expecting a long stakeout. Young men loitered on the corner selling drugs. The street was rundown, dirty and dangerous. It wouldn't be long before everyone knew where the two cops were.

"Is this the right place?" Roger Mills asked his partner, glancing through the grimy windshield.

"It has to be, that was David Prince," Sam Trunce said, gesturing with his coffee cup over the steering wheel in the direction of the closing door.

"I didn't get a good look."

"I sat through four days of trial. I know what the puke looks like. The only honest testimony he gave was his name. Besides, you know it was a done deal when the judge threw out the dope we found. No, that's him."

"Now, you can't blame the judge. You did run Prince off the road and beat him with the evidence in plain sight of a bunch of witnesses. Now don't get me wrong, I loved it, but generally good police work doesn't involve clubbing a suspect with a suitcase full of heroin and yelling, 'book em Dano' when the uniforms show up. That didn't play well in court," Mills said, wagging a finger at his partner and smiling wryly.

"Okay, granted, I did get carried away, but he did have several pounds of a 'powdery substance' in the trunk."

"Technically he did, but when you first saw him, you only had a hunch that he had dope in the trunk, and that's what you told the judge. You can't be so blunt; you need to massage the truth a little during probable cause hearings. You know, give the judge an 'accurate' description of the totality of the circumstances."

"I hate that damn word, technically. Technically, this asshole traffics massive quantities of narcotics and would sell to nursery school kids if he could."

"Well buddy, one thing I know, is that you can't beat a guy with a case full of dope in the middle of the city and expect to call it a good bust," Mills said kicking aside a hamburger wrapper grimacing at the general disarray inside the vehicle. "How did you get so big and strong eating all this crap?"

"What? This is stakeout food. Besides you can get away with it if you go to the gym," Sam said gently poking his older partner's modest paunch.

"Yah right, and your car smells like a gym."

"Maybe, but it's time to take a look," Sam said reaching for the door handle. "This time, I guarantee I'm going to see some probable cause when I peek in the doorway."

"Sam, as your friend, approaching a significant retirement milestone, you need to see something concrete in there. Giant piles of dope in plain sight would be best."

"I learned my lesson the last time, Roger, Scout's honor," Sam said, holding up his fingers in the Boy Scout salute, punctuated with a grin.

"I guarantee that you ain't no Boy Scout," Mills said with a chuckle.

"I was a scout in the army."

"Remember, you can't pull your 'Special Forces' crap on everybody you don't like, Sammy."

"I'll be careful. If it looks like it's iffy, I'll let you know before I go in and you can call for backup. If nothing's going on, I'll slide back out and we'll pick him up another day."

"Okay, I'll play along. I'll be the doorman on the other side. No cowboy shit. I'm too close to retirement to stand in front of the chief's desk with my hat in my hand, trying to explain why I went along with some bonehead move. You go check it out and I'll call it in and give em heads up in case we need it."

"See you in the middle, partner." Sam said sliding off into the shadow of the nearest wall concealing his intent from the few people passing by in the street.

Sam ghosted along the side of the building and into a tight passageway, moving carefully, determined to do this one by the book. He came up to a door that was slightly ajar and looked inside. There were three men in the room, the man he'd followed in and a shorter one, taking turns beating a third guy tied to a chair. Sam recognized the smaller man as Martin Thompson, a thug who had beaten a murder rap years ago, one of Prince's nastier enforcers. Sam positioned his body so that he could keep an eye on Thompson. Prince stepped back out of view as Thompson moved in to take his turn.

"Do him," Prince muttered like he was ordering a cup of coffee.

Smiling, Thompson snarled, "Look David, this mofo got blood on my sleeve." He drew a pistol from his belt and began to turn the gun on the man slumped in the chair. As Thompson pulled back the hammer, Sam ripped his 45 out of his shoulder holster, slamming open the door as he crashed through it. Without hesitation he fired catching Thompson in the chest as he swung his gun in Sam's direction. The big .45 caliber slugs hit Thompson like sledge hammers swatting him back with their concussive force. Prince jammed his hand into his coat pocket reaching for his weapon.

"Please do," Sam said as he leveled his gun at Prince's torso. "We can finish this right now, and save the tax payers a lot of money."

Prince slowly raised his hands away from his sides holding them at shoulder level as he glared at Sam with a mixture of hate and indecision, furious that he'd been caught.

"Move your hands and I shoot you in the knee first. You won't like that, I promise," Sam said edging closer towards Prince as he kicked Thompson's gun out of the immediate area with his shoe. "Now, Mister Prince, what's a nice man like you doing trying to kill a guy in my city?" Sam said, keeping his focus on Prince as Thompson's body jerked and laid still. "He's done," Sam said tipping his head in Thompson's direction as he reached with his left hand drawing a second gun from a waist holster strapped to his right side. He trained both on the man in front of him.

"I owe you cop, I get the chance, you are one dead motherfucker!" Prince said through a sneer. Almost imperceptibly, his posture changed as his eyes darted over in the direction of a side door.

At the last second, Sam realized something was wrong. Had he been alone, Prince might have tried to run when Sam burst into the room or get to his weapon more quickly. He was not alone. Through a door to Sam's left, three men ran into the room with their guns pointed at him. They hesitated, seeing Prince's hands in the air.

"Well, cop man, what are you going to do now?" Prince said beginning to lower his hands, glancing over Sam's left shoulder.

"Lower your hands and I'll shoot you now, and not in the knee," Sam said boring his eyes into Prince's. "I may be surrounded, Hoss but that just means we've got a decision to make," Sam said, adjusting his aim. "I recommend that the boys behind me take it easy. I didn't just stroll in here alone."

"Nice try. I've got guys on the corner and if a bunch of po-lice were outside we'd know."

"I got in here," Sam said.

"Yah and look at your dead ass now, asshole," Prince hissed through a twisted smile.

"It doesn't have to go down that way. I will get you and a couple of those boys," Sam said gesturing with his head. That's right boys, I'm Special Forces. I will kill some of you. I guarantee that. I may get popped, but I will get you."

The men confronting Sam glanced at each other and looked at Prince, expecting him to make a move or say something. They weren't in a hurry to start shooting and Sam could sense their hesitation.

The drug dealer looked carefully at the big cop pointing an equally big gun at his head. The cop wasn't scared in the least. Obviously, this wasn't the first time a gun had been pointed at him. He counted up the prison time in his head for the massive quantity of heroin in the next room, then for attempted murder and resisting arrest. He really didn't care if his men got away, he could buy more, but he wanted to get away himself and take his drugs with him. He instantly made a decision and dove to the side.

Sam spun and moved, shifting his weight and torso to throw off the aim of the men behind him. He saw three and fired at two of them, and fired a shot to spoil the aim of the third. They fired back wildly and most of the shots missed, most of them. Sam was caught in his upper chest and leg simultaneously by large caliber bullets. He had felt the impact of the bullets without pain. He rolled and came up with his Sig-Sauer and his .45. He got off several shots and took out the two men who had been in front of him. He was just slow enough so that one of them got off a round that hit him square in the cheek and went through, knocking him back onto the floor.

Everyone in the room was down. Smoke hung in the air, stinking of gunpowder and dead men. On his back, Sam rolled his head the best he could to check for movement. That was about all he could do. He saw the other men were down and motionless, Prince wasn't among them. Shit, he missed his man again. He reached up feeling a tear ripped through the right side of his cheek. Blood ran down his chin onto his neck as he tried to count the number of holes in him. His head was wet with blood, as he felt a pool spreading out slowly from his upper body. Briefly his mind focused when he heard Mill's huge Dirty Harry cannon go off three times, followed by a big thud and then silence.

"You lose, Prince!" he spat out through his torn mouth, blood spraying out with each word.

Mills ran into the room and saw Sam on the floor covered in blood.

He yelled "Officer down!" into a hand radio as he hurried to Sam's side holstering his pistol seeing the dead men scattered around the room.

"You big dumb bastard. You better not die on me, soldier!" Mills said as he dropped to his knees, tearing open Sam's shirt.

Sam turned his head and looked up at Roger. He heard him, but it was like a whisper from far away. He knew he had to concentrate on staying awake. He could feel Mill's hands on him, working to stop the hemorrhaging. Roger never talked about his time as a medic in Vietnam, not even to his partner.

"Sorry Roger, looks like I fucked up again," Sam said reaching out to touch Roger's leg. He felt like he was deflating and Roger looked like the only thing solid in the room.

"The choppers are coming, big man, a bed with sheets and nurses. You stay with me. It's no big thing." Mills was somewhere else a long time past. His hands were skillful and practiced as he worked to keep Sam alive.

It seemed funny to Sam how the words didn't seem remotely out of place. Mill's tone was soothing and comforting, like a brother or a best friend. He relaxed a little, but knew he was bad. God damn drug dealers, Sam thought.

"Tell my parents I love them. John Trunce, Patience Missouri," Sam said slipping down. He looked up at Mills and saw a mixture of compassion and resolve. Maybe he'd die, maybe he wouldn't he thought. He didn't seem to mind.

"No you don't Sam. No way you're leaving me here. You don't get to die today," Roger said looking directly into Sam's eyes.

Emergency medical personnel and several uniformed officers crashed into the room. Sam slid over the invisible edge. Mills was still at his side when it all went dark.

CHAPTER
ONE

Sam bolted up in his bed; a sheen of sweat covered him as he remembered where he was, home, and not shot up on some dirty floor in Detroit. He had the dream much less often but it still came.

Sam swung his legs over the side of the bed and counted his blessings. He had had enough of sleep and dreaming for one night. He pulled on a t-shirt over his scars and looked out his window, squinting into the Missouri sunshine. He knew he had a lot to be thankful for. The doctors had been great, but it had been Roger Mills who had saved his life. While Sam was still in the hospital, Roger had put in his retirement papers. He had visited Sam often, and when Sam moved back to Missouri, Roger kept in touch, even coming to visit him once in a while in that big Winnebago of his.

Outside Sam's modest home, the air hung thick and heavy. It was mid-morning and the oppressive heat would only get worse. The buzz of the cicadas gave the dark woods an eerie, prehistoric feel. Growth crept everywhere up to the curtain of the highway and around every post, mail box, and tree.

Sam walked out of his bedroom and looked around his empty home. It was full of things, but didn't feel like a home. He was alone except for an ancient, scrawny cat that made a mournful howl as Sam lumbered into the kitchen and attacked the coffee pot. Sam scratched the cat's ears, he had a soft spot for cast offs and runaways. Some days he felt like one himself.

"Mangy rat. Today's the day for the dog food factory," he declared, smoothing down the old tom cat's fur.

The cat had been his girlfriend's, the girlfriend who now lived somewhere else with someone else. She had left the sorry looking animal behind like an unwanted gift you can't return.

All coffee was good first thing in the morning as long as it was black and corrosively strong. The older he got the less he felt like blasting into action. Since the shooting it seemed like he needed more time than he used to wake the hell up and get oriented.

The cat rubbed up against Sam's leg mewing at him and varying his pitch like he was trying to speak.

"You're probably right kitty, I'm just getting old and worn out and should probably just hang out with you for the day," Sam said tickling the cat's ears.

Sam walked out onto his porch, sat on a wooden swing and looked out onto the day. There had been a time recently when he met every day with optimism and a sense of adventure. After the shooting, that spark had been slow to come back. He was getting to that age when he knew he wanted something to bring his life together. What that was continued to elude him. He looked at the old clock thermometer hanging next to the door. It was time to go to work. He got up and went inside to the bathroom. He glanced at himself in the mirror and decided that he looked like a bouncer. One certainty he had discovered, was that you just can't change your genetics, at least not yet. Until then he'd make some effort to keep healthy, do some running or hiking and lift weights. Being shot and coming close to death put vanity and health into immediate perspective. Well screw it, he thought, time for work.

Sam wandered into his sparsely furnished bedroom. He wasn't much interested in décor and seemed to spend more time outside than in. He'd picked out his furniture in about an hour, all from the same store.

As he dressed for work, he felt a little slower and thought, the only thing about me that is quick these days is my temper. He was pissed off a lot. Maybe that was an age thing, too. No wonder generals and admirals were older and ill-tempered. He remembered meeting an old WW II Navy

Captain once, who had been about his age during the war. Out of curiosity Sam asked him, "What's the first thing you do if an enemy ship is steaming towards you over the horizon?"

"Sink the bastard," was the reply. That pretty much summed up Sam's feelings toward the world today. Something needed to happen to push him out of this funk. Maybe today was the day for moving on. In his experience, life changing events came when you least expected.

Sam stepped to the railing of his porch and gazed out across the long hill in front and far off into the distance, where he could see the land just shy of the Mississippi, but not the river itself. He knew it was there. It always was when he went to find it. Like many people who live near water, he went to check on it from time to time. There were always people fishing down by the river. Sam liked to see his old friends, meet new people and talk fishing.

Sam walked down the length of his porch. It was nice and wide to keep the sun from blasting it all day. Most summer days, the second he stepped outside his door he was drenched with sweat. The humidity was stagger-ing. The only relief was the thunderstorms which came with a ferocity that was both exhilarating and scary. Sam had built his modest home, up the hill and away from the river the creek became when the sky opened up. With the summer vegetation growing over everything and the constant sound of insects, the area Sam lived in was all but jungle. If it was a choice between hot in the summer or cold in the winter he'd take hot every time. The winters during his years as a cop in Detroit had torpedoed any roman-tic notions of winter wonderlands he may have mistakenly entertained. Winters in the upper Midwest were life threatening, at least to a Missouri country boy. What had he been thinking about when he followed an old army buddy into the Detroit police force?

Sam walked out onto his lawn and over to his squad car. It was as close to a tank as you could get. When starting up it sounded like the green flag drop at the Indy 500. Everything close that could, fled. The raw power made him smile as he tore off in the direction of town. Sam punched it on a lonely stretch of road and the car roared like a tractor pulling full throttle at a county fair. He pretty much had to hold the steering wheel straight. It had what he called 'Armstrong' steering, no power anything. Sometimes it was a wrestling match, but it was just how he liked it. It was a car you avoided flooring in a turn. It was truly a beast, announcing that the man behind the wheel was no Barney Fife.

Being in no particular hurry, Sam thought he'd meander around a little and check on the general status of things in Patience. Sam did a lot of cruising just to keep track of what was going on and who was doing what. He liked to drive and hated sitting in an office. Since his days as a beat cop and a detective in Detroit he hated being cooped up doing paper work. This way he could say "Howdy" to the people on a daily basis, whether they were normal, borderline, or downright nuts.

When his other life went to hell in Michigan, he came back home to find some peace. There was little in the way of crime in Patience and that was all right by him. He'd seen enough lunatic violent crime to last several lifetimes: too many murder investigations, rapes, and arson. Every type of violence men and women can do to each other. Patience had its own set of unique situations and Sam handled each as they came. His constituents either loved him or were terrified of him.

Sam loved the quiet clean streets and countryside of Patience. Everything seemed in its place and reminded him of the simpler times of his youth. Nothing was simple in adult life. He remembered how hectic and disorganized things had been chasing murderers around Detroit, the politics, the dirty cops and the sense of helplessness that fouled everything in the high crime areas. Patience was as far away from that as you could get. He intended to keep it that way.

As he drove by the city park, Sam noticed a gray Dodge parked alongside the road. He'd seen it there and a few other places children frequented around town. He'd been patient and watched for a pattern to develop.

"Damn it," Sam muttered to himself. "No second chance this time."

He pulled the squad a ways up the road and unbelted his pistol, leaving it under the front seat. Few of his duties in Patience required a firearm. Besides, if he was correct, the perpetrator he expected to encounter would be little trouble. He walked quickly and quietly up to a clump of trees and brush next to an area where the younger children played in the park. Sam saw a couple of kids on swing sets and a merry-go-round playing happily, while their mothers or sitters watched them, glancing up regularly from their books or papers.

As he neared the bushes he pulled a tiny digital camera from his pocket and crept forward. Eight years in Special Forces had taught him stealth, and he liked to sneak up on bad guys. Nothing like when the hero walks right up, plain as day, courageous and exposed. No damn way. You sneak up on the bad guy and take his ass out. Then you stand up and are the hero. All you have to do is be shot at once to know that's true.

As Sam got closer, he saw a middle-aged man crouched in the bushes watching the children intently. From time to time he would reach down into his pants. It looked like he was going to take some time with that, so Sam took about twenty pictures: hand in pants, hand out of pants, licking his lips, mumbling to himself, an all-together sickening display. Not wanting to spoil the moment, Sam crept back to his car to make sure that the pictures were saved for later reference. He then walked back into the bushes plain as day making as much noise as possible. Whistling tunelessly Sam walked right up to the man, who was quickly trying to organize the front of his pants. As the man spun around he quickly said, "Good morning sheriff, my little dog ran…"

Sam hated people who preyed on kids in any way. While he considered the implications of just grabbing his gun and blasting the pervert, he came up with something more fun with less potential for litigation. Sam just smiled and without breaking stride kicked him casually in the crotch. Then he balled up his big hand and clubbed him on top of the head.

"Morning Deacon. Fine morning, isn't it?" Sam boomed as he stood over the groaning man. "Great day for a move, wouldn't you say? I've noticed you seem restless lately and there's nothing better for a twitchy foot than seeing what else the fine world has to offer."

Deacon Robert Jones looked up at Sam and unwisely tried to speak. At that point Sam just put his size thirteen extra wide down on the unfortunate man's head and applied a little pressure.

"Now, don't try to thank me. Helping people is my business and my advice is always helpful. You've lived in the state for many years. You need a change of scenery. That's just what the doctor ordered. I promise to keep in touch. We can take pictures and send them to each other, just like these." Sam moved his foot just enough for the man to see the pictures on the screen of the digital camera. "Like 'em?" Sam yelled. "I thought you might. Now I'll keep these as a reminder of your great ecumenical service to our community, but they're special to me so I'll just keep them myself. Now, if you decide to hang around, say, more than twenty four hours, I'll share them with everyone so they can all enjoy your smiling face and line up to thank you in person."

Sam looked down for a response. As the man nodded repeatedly, he reached down with one hand and pulled him to his feet, brushed him off and adjusted his clothing. Nothing like a reasonable response to a problem, Sam thought. Catch a guy red-handed, beat him some, then threaten him with a promise of a catastrophe that he knows will happen, and often times people will see things your way.

"I'm sick, Sheriff," the Deacon croaked as he cowered in front of Sam, blubbering his woes. Sam wanted to slap some back bone into him but realized this man of the cloth probably would never have any.

"The best medicine is the open road. You should see a doctor when you get there. Send me his name. I'm sure I'll hear from you within the month." Sam smiled and flicked open a slender stiletto and began to clean his fingernails with the tip.

"Of course, of course, as soon as possible," the man said.

Sam pointed out of the bushes with the knife and followed the man out as he limped and sort of hopped a little bit. Sam waved as the Deacon dropped into his car and he slid into the squad. Sam considered that while the man had committed a lewd act, it was a petty offense. He had no confirmed reports of similar conduct on the part of the Deacon, just his own suspicions. The people of Patience might question the sudden move but Sam was sure the Deacon could conjure up a sick relative somewhere. People didn't want the truth about this one, better to toss the rotten apple out of the barrel and get on with life. Knowing that one of your spiritual leaders peeks at little kids while engaging in solitary sin can be disconcerting.

Once Sam knew where the man landed, he'd inform local law enforcement to keep an eye on him. Charging him with a petty misdemeanor wouldn't stop him, but the fear of knowing the police were keeping an eye on him would.

Sam sat in the car and listened to his stomach rumble. He decided crime fighting could be done on a full stomach just as well as an empty one. He pulled out into traffic and headed downtown.

CHAPTER
TWO

S am stopped off at the local diner, Sheila's, and pulled up to the curb. He'd been going to the diner since he was a kid. Every table, chair, cup and saucer was original, worn but clean and serviceable. The linoleum had faded to an almost pastel color. There were small diners like Sheila's all over the country. The décor went with the familiar smells of people, grease and home cooking. He walked in it was to a mixed chorus of "Hey Sheriff," "Hey Sam," "Hey Boy," "Son," "Sammy." They all knew him and only called him sheriff on official business.

"Howdy y'all," he said.

Sam loved those words. They were wonderfully collective and suited every occasion. He'd always been harassed for his country choice of words up north. Conversation in the south was often accomplished with a few choice words and sometimes not even that.

He walked over to the lunch counter, clapped a few people on the back and lowered himself onto a stool. Carl Smith nodded in his direction, and Sam nodded back. That tiny nod was universal. It said, "I see you, I acknowledge your presence, and you deserve at least the expenditure of one calorie of my energy resources to move my neck ½ an inch." Farmers like Smith were the backbone of the community. They had been working the land for years before Sam was born. Sam had met Carl's wife Alma some years ago. She didn't have squat to say either. He'd gotten a glance though. He often wondered if these people just sat at home and nodded and glanced at one another after the chores were done. Then he remembered that they raised fourteen kids. They must have been damn good at nodding and glancing.

Sheila Trempford walked out of the kitchen and over to where Sam was sitting. She didn't glance at all; she beamed. Everyone knew she had the hots for Sam. She liked Sam's rugged good looks, blue-green eyes, a little rough around the edges.

For his part, Sam wasn't looking for a girlfriend, and certainly not somebody he liked as much as Sheila. He couldn't bear to screw up their friendship.

Sam looked over at Sheila and liked everything he saw. She had gentle country good looks, a nimble mind and a smile for everyone. It wasn't the cooking that made the place so popular. People swore that being around Sheila just made the food taste better.

Sheila walked over to Sam, her apron tied behind her back in a way that accentuated her curves. Some people can pull the apron thing off and some can't, Sam thought as he tried to think of some smart-alec thing to say.

"Potatoes or Oatmeal?" she asked, knowing Sam was pretty predictable.

"First things first. Today I'm with the health department and I have to say, you do look healthy!"

"A man dedicated to public service, passably good-looking, and generous with his compliments! What else could you want?" Sheila bantered back.

"More coffee," somebody said.

"Jack Wilson, you drink so damn much of my coffee that you should just call ahead and get it in a bucket and take it all at once and spare me the daily hours of seeing your sorry face in here licking it up drop by drop."

That had done it. There was a huge laugh around the lunch counter, Jack Wilson the loudest.

When Sam had stopped laughing and shaking his head he said, "Potatoes would be great."

A few minutes later a mixing bowl of potatoes appeared in front of him, along with a pepper grinder and butter. Sam added the butter, some pepper and a healthy dose of Tabasco.

Sheila came around the counter and slid in next to him.

"Anything exciting today, Sammy?" she asked.

"I have to go out to see Carl Koots, problem with his neighbor."

"Carl the chicken fucker?" Mike Vance, the school janitor, asked sitting two seats down the counter.

"Now, there's no proof he ever fucked a chicken," Sam said earnestly. His little voice said "I can't believe that I used the words chicken fucker" in a serious conversation." There were a few things about rural living that fell into the absurd category. At least the lack of barnyard animals in big cities kept the practice of bestiality indoors.

"Well, that's not what I heard," Vance stated resolutely as if that settled the discussion. Sam closed his eyes and shook his head like he was the only sane man in a community of crazies.

"People, it's 2001. Who cares whether a man has a thing for chickens or not? Maybe he's a recluse who somebody decided years ago enjoyed all aspects of chicken husbandry, from courtship to mating to eating. Shouldn't our town have everything a town needs? You know a doctor, a banker, a lawyer and the celebrated position of chicken fucker?" Sam said sarcastically.

Sheila was pinching her leg and biting her lip to keep from laughing. She was shaking and her eyes were absolutely on fire. Sam looked at her and was instantly affected. There is nothing funnier than trying not to laugh with somebody else. Especially a pretty girl, he thought. They'd almost made it when somebody started crowing like a rooster. Sam and Sheila lost it together. Life was good.

After breakfast and a cruise through town, Sam pulled onto a grown over gravel road and drove up to a small, well-kept log home. He noticed a large garden and a couple of chicken barns. He glanced into one and was turning to walk to the house when a voice said, "I bet you're wondering if I think I can fuck them all."

An older man stepped up to Sam. He stood ram-rod straight, his face weathered from the outdoors. There was no old age stoop, only a balanced readiness to the man's body. He was lean, and moved well for a man his age, but he was no spring chicken. Sam looked into Carl's eyes and didn't dare crack a smile.

"No sir." The look on the man's face made Sam feel small. That's when he noticed the American flag fluttering in the wind next to a small garden out back.

"Sometimes I run around here without clothes on and once some clown in a delivery truck saw me carrying a chicken. Now if I was going to have relations with some animal it wouldn't be a chicken. They'd just squawk about it."

The older man smiled and they both laughed.

"Young man, I don't give a damn what anyone thinks about me, except for a very few men. Now you look familiar."

"I'm Sam Trunce."

"John's boy?"

"Yes sir."

"He should have brought you around."

"Dad visits you?"

"He better, I saved his ass in France. He talks about you though."

"Sorry, I didn't realize that he knew you. He keeps quiet about the people he knew in the wars."

"Three wars, hard to believe, one was enough for me. There are few soldiers like John Trunce. Forty years airborne!" Carl said with pride. "Now, what can I do for you, Sheriff?"

"Well, Mr. Koots, I understand there's some kind of fence dispute, with your neighbor, Mr. Dupree."

"You mean the goat fondler?"

"Well, I guess if people call you chicken fucker, you're not going to like it much."

"Well, he may not be a real goat fondler but he's pissing me off just the same."

Great, then let's sink the bastard, Sam thought as he nodded in response to Koot's statement.

"I had words with him over it. He got his cattle back in when I fired a few rounds into the air. He understood that."

"Well, he kind of mentioned it, Mr. Koots. You seem calm now, let's go see Mr. Dupree and see if we can get this thing under control."

Both men walked over to the squad and Sam drove the short distance over to the next farm. The house was an old clapboard with a fresh coat of paint. There was a nice garden, a barn, a pen with cattle and a small flower garden with a little headstone. The American flag fluttered in the breeze right next to it. As Koots exited the car he immediately noticed the flag.

"Sam, how old is this guy?"

"I think he's about your age, sir."

Koots nodded and followed Sam up to the front door. Sam knocked and it was quickly answered by an older man, standing tall and straight. He looked right past Sam and addressed Koots.

"You gonna shoot? Because I will shoot back."

It wasn't a threat or delivered in a macho boasting way, it was a statement of fact.

"No, sir."

"Then I suppose you men want to come in?"

"If we could, Mr. Dupree," Sam's Southern manners told him not to come right to the point. Men of this generation would get to the point in good time. These were Southern gentlemen and manners were expected. Sam liked it that way. It gave a little more order to a world where there was enough confusion, enough meanness.

Dupree moved aside and Koots and Sam walked into the entry way. The home was neatly kept. There was a smell of freshly baked cookies in the air and a clean, homemade rug under their feet, and a little dog curled up in the corner. It was a place where haste and hurry were left at the door.

Dupree showed them through the entry way into the sitting room. As he walked into the room Koots passed an upright cabinet with medals, pictures, and a few maps displayed on top.

"Were you with the 101st at Bastonne, Mr. Dupree?" Koots asked.

"Nobody remembers that. Yah, I was there." Dupree said in a faraway wistful voice.

"Me too," Koots said quietly.

"What! I didn't know you were Airborne."

Without hesitation, the men walked towards each other, embraced, and met like old friends who started talking a mile a minute.

Sam's jaw hit the floor. These men had just traveled through time. They weren't pushing eighty anymore, they were fire-eating Airborne Rangers again.

Sam sighed a little in relief. Apparently neither man had any carnal designs on the goat and chicken populations of Patience County. If they did, Sam was certain that they would restrict their activities to the animals they raised for breeding purposes. Sam laughed out loud at his own bad pun, thinking how dangerous random rumors could be regardless of how far-fetched.

Sam said, "I'll leave you guys to work it out then."

Neither man seemed to notice at all, so Sam just walked quietly out the door and over to his car. People are amazing, he thought. Not only had he brought two neighbors together, but he was sure these guys would be best of friends. Even though he hadn't really done much, it made him feel damn good to see it. The exchange had been just the thing to see the sunny side of things.

Sam jumped back into the squad and headed to the Sheriff's station for his routine check in. His office was housed in an old concrete building on the far end of town from the shops and business offices. He passed friends on the street, making the required head nod or finger wave. He and his buddies often joked about it when they passed a farmer on a tractor and got the single digit lifted off the steering wheel salute. He smiled when he pulled up to the squat ugly concrete and cinder block building that looked more like an errant fortification than a city office. Rommel would have approved, Sam thought as he got out of the vehicle. There were places where the walls were three feet thick and rebar reinforced.

Lisa Coleman, the receptionist, greeted Sam as he walked in the door.

"What are people doing to each other today?" It was the same thing Sam asked her every day, always hoping for the same answer.

"Nothing new today, but your mother called to remind you about Sunday dinner."

"Thanks Lisa, she always does."

The informal, Patience County Traveling Pot Luck, had been a tradition dating back to the civil war. Many of the same families still attended. Sam's father showed up after he started dating Sam's mother. At their third pot luck together, Sam's parents snuck off together down to a nearby swimming hole. Skinny dipping remained one of his parent's favorite activities together. Sam's uncles hadn't liked that very much and Sam's father hadn't bothered to put his clothes back on when he took Sam's three uncles on. The young men fought to a standstill and an understanding. After that, Sam's uncles kept all other suitors away. That skinny paratrooper was tough as hell and he was their brother now. The fight was still laughed and joked about.

There were always lots of people and a huge feed moving from house to house among their friends and family. By the end of the week at least a dozen people had reminded him of where it was. They were there when he left Patience and there when he came back.

Sam rambled back through the neatly organized sheriff's station, with its offices in the front and few jail cells in the back. There was little need to hold people at the station, as the courthouse had a separate detention facility for those offenders serving county jail time or waiting to appear in court. That arrangement allowed Sam and his deputies to attend to their duties and not have to take care of prisoners. He didn't think most people needed to be held anyway. If they were violent and had to be held, the courthouse was best. If not, Sam could always provide them with many good reasons to leave his county, very few of which were in any handbook anywhere. Sam checked his messages and the duty roster. Satisfied, he headed back out the door.

"I hereby declare the world safe for democracy," Sam announced.

"It is until you get back in that squad, sheriff," Lisa joked.

Sam jumped back into his car and drove a few blocks over to TJ's Auto to gas up. TJ was a close friend of Sam's father John and had been with him in Vietnam in a unit that saw more than its share of combat. After the war, TJ kind of drifted around and got into stupid trouble, drinking and fighting. He was a tough kid from East L.A., and had been born into one of the tougher gangs. He often joked he'd been in combat all his life. He did some jail time, dried up for a while and then repeated the pattern. John had heard about TJ's troubles and went to find him. John knew that TJ just lacked a sense of purpose, having come from less than nothing before the war, some inner city slum. When the war was over he had nowhere to go and nothing to do. That was a perfect recipe to get any man in trouble. TJ was a natural mechanic and had learned about engines as a child in the shop of a decent man in his neighborhood who he still called his uncle. The man was long dead, but when TJ was temporarily stumped or couldn't figure something out, he'd say "I bet ol' Uncle Gary would have figured it out already." Sam had driven all manner of vehicles in the military and in police life, from the most rugged military Humvees to luxury cars that cost in the hundreds of thousands of dollars, but he liked his squad the best. It was a 1990 Ford Crown Victoria, one of the old interceptors. TJ had taken one purchased at an auction in another county and altered it some. It was capable of producing over 800 horsepower on a modified frame and could go at least 160 mph as long as you didn't want to turn. It had bullet proof everything and had solid rubber tires. It drank gas like a dragster and could be geared low enough to tow a river barge if need be. The engine was air, water, and oil cooled, turbo charged with ram air injection. It was downright silly and that's why Sam loved it.

When he pulled in TJ gave him a wry grin and shook his head almost imperceptibly.

"Fill 'er up," Sam sang out as he jumped out of the vehicle and clapped TJ on the back, "with the special juice."

"Special juice my ass, Sam. I told you before racing fuel is for racing."

"Then let's go racing," Sam winked. He knew TJ was the man to see. When TJ drove one of his antique honeys, everybody looked.

"I'd feel safer in the jungle with the enemy than on the back of a bicycle with you," TJ said smiling and wagging a finger at Sam.

"You have a point."

It wasn't that Sam was a bad driver, but in the last four years he had sunk the squad twice and on two separate occasions had landed in a cornfield in pursuit of a suspect. It was times like these that made him glad that TJ was his friend. The squad had a distinctive throttle sound when it kicked down. On a still night the sound carried. No other car was like it. When people heard it they knew that Sam was on patrol. It was one of those echoes in the night, like a train off in the distance. People told him they liked hearing the squad, knowing he was on the job.

The squad had a normal, bench-style front seat and two separate seats in the back. One for a normal sized passenger and one that looked like it was made for a giant.

There were so many dents in the squad that TJ just replaced the shell every so often, so that from the outside it looked at least halfway normal. Its color was mostly black and tan. The lights on top were bolted to the heavy duty frame and needed to be replaced constantly. Sam had cleaned Patience County up when he returned. Nobody seemed to care about the repair bills.

TJ hopped into the car and drove it around back where the stash of high octane racing fuel was kept. Sam walked to the front of the station and onto the small porch where two ancient men intermittently played checkers and ribbed one another mercilessly. They were the same two men who had been there when Sam left at eighteen and they were still there when he came home at forty two. They looked the same, spoke the same and still called him boy, unless it was 'official'. Then they called him Sheriff. They were both a little crazy and convinced that the Catholics in town were trying to get them. They never offered an explanation as to their religious persecution and Sam wisely didn't ask, but he never ignored them. They saw everything and seemed to have crystal clear recall for details concerning people 'not from around here'.

"Howdy, gents," Sam said.

"Boy," was the simultaneous reply.

Sam walked into the shop and the old wooden floor creaked as he walked over to the cooler to get an IBC Root Beer and a bag of cheese puffs. They had been his favorite snack since childhood, when he rode his bike to town or cut through the woods with Nathan avoiding his chores. Another man had owned the filling station then, but it never seemed to change. The interior had the same slanted greasy floor, dirty cracked display cases and tired old Snap-on-Tool calendars on the walls it had thirty years ago. Sam put a couple of dollars on the counter and walked out back to where TJ was fueling the squad.

TJ finished topping off the tank and Sam jumped in and fired up the engine. The engine sounded like a spitfire starting up. Sam smiled and TJ said, "Sunday dinner at your parents."

It was Sam's turn for the wry smile and incredulous shake of his head. TJ laughed right out loud. It was always fun to hear TJ's explosion of mirth and glee. He was a relatively new conscript to Sunday pot luck, having only been around for twenty years or so.

CHAPTER
THREE

Sam drove the rumbling squad into Nathan Harper's rutted dirt driveway and came to a stop next to a barn that had once been red. He climbed out and took an appreciative sniff of the air. Nathan's garden was bursting with growth. Large tomatoes were forming on his vines, which had been staked recently, and fragrant tiny grapes were developing among shiny leaves clinging to the arbor that arched by the barn door.

Sam saw that Nathan's big farm truck was gone, more than likely making deliveries or hauling packages of the home grown specialty organic products Nathan shipped to restaurants all over the region.

To make sure, Sam walked over to the front door, stuck his head inside and called out. Not hearing a response, Sam figured there was nobody home. Sam and Nathan had free reign in each other's homes. They were closer than brothers and didn't bother with asking each other permission for much of anything. Sam walked over to one of Nathan's barns where the makeshift weight room was set up.

Sam ducked into the barn just as a couple of mice scurried across the floor in search of some discarded grain sack or other morsel. There was dirt and dust everywhere except on the heavy bench press, squat rack and pull up bar. It was an old fashioned weight pit. No frills. Over in the corner was some of the equipment Nathan used. One was a welded barbell made of a four inch thick iron bar connected to enormous old-fashioned steel tractor wheels. They were heavy enough so that the bar bent considerably under their weight. Nathan was much too broad for a conventional Olympic bar. It didn't much matter, as he couldn't fit enough weight on one any way. Sam used on old Olympic weight set they'd trained with for years.

Nathan's bench presses were done with massive iron barbells that an old time blacksmith made for him in exchange for some chickens and that venom Nathan called moonshine. Sam tried to lift one of the bells just off the floor. He could do it, but it would take two good men to get one into the back of a pickup. Sam was gone when they were made, but the story was that the old smith, applying the wisdom of his years, used a skid-steer loader to deliver them.

Sam's workout was basic, squats, bench presses, and pull-ups; that was it. Nathan and Sam believed in exercise in moderation. It was easier to make themselves do it. Sam's real physical talent was his ability to move with loose, fluid ferocity, born of countless hours of running through the woods, swimming in creeks and spending most of his younger years exploring the wild areas near his home. Sam would still often take off for hours into the woods alone, climbing trees, running and just rambling about. When he was young his parents once saw him outside lying face down on the ground with his arms outstretched like he was hugging the earth. Sam could always rejuvenate himself by spending time alone anywhere in the wild. Sometimes old man Trunce would say, "Sam's gone walkabout again," for like an aborigine, he had the same uncanny sense of direction and the same wanderlust.

The Trunces and the Harpers were great friends. Nathan, like his father, was a botanist. His father had a PhD. but Nathan was a farmer. While his father taught at the university, Nathan was interested in the practical side of the science. By the time he was in his teens he had spent long hours working with his father doing sophisticated research. When he went to university, he tested out of all but the highest level courses. Nathan spent about eighteen months taking all of the required courses and graduated. He did so more to please his father than himself. Dr. Harper was an academic, and while he didn't insist that his son obtain a degree, he was openly proud when he did. Nathan graduated with honors and had the pick of any graduate school of his choice, but he chose farming as his continuing education. Dr. Harper was a decent farmer and a respected scientist, but Nathan could grow things by wiggling his toes in the soil. It was Nathan, who the other farmers called when they had questions. They generally said "could you ask Dr. Harper and Nathan to call around?" Nathan and Dr. Harper both read every journal of importance that came out in the field of botany and conducted all manner of research at the university and at the farm. Nathan was always included in the credits of every paper published. He was a natural organic farmer, and had great interest in natural forms of pest and weed control, crop rotation, and the combination of species to deter insects and disease. Nathan wanted to be able to help feed the world without poisoning it.

Nathan's father had been in John Trunce's ranger unit in Vietnam as a young officer. He had joined the military in an effort to attempt to control his destiny, as he saw many of his African American friends and relatives drafted into the general infantry and told where to go. As many of the men who ended up in elite units, Joseph Harper wanted to be surrounded by the best and brightest. He thought his ability to survive the war would be improved. Many black men at the time, regardless of their aptitude, ended up in combat units. Joseph's deferral for college was over; he'd graduated and he thought it would be best to go in as an officer and to try to save some lives if he could. Joseph lived with his family in rural Mississippi and most of the young men from the poorest areas of the state seemed to be going off to war. Not only did he not feel different from these young men simply because he was intellectually and physically gifted, they were his family and community and he had to stick with them. To survive poverty, people in families and long standing friendships rely on one another to get along. There was a common struggle and suffering, at least where Joseph grew up. While everyone was proud of Joseph, they were even prouder when he enlisted and went to Officer Training School. Joseph had some ideas about defending his country, freedom and the flag, but for him it was more personal. His friends and cousins had to go, so he had to go. The idea that somebody else might have to fight if he stayed didn't sit well with him. His personal faith and sense of duty to others just wouldn't allow it. Besides, Joseph told his family and friends, since he was an All- American running back at the University of Mississippi, he could outrun anything the enemy threw at him. He had a shot at professional football and a stellar academic career, but left them behind to fulfill his responsibilities as he saw them.

Joseph joined the army, excelled, and went to Officer Training School where he excelled again and ended up in Airborne Ranger Training. It was there where he first encountered Colonel John Trunce. Colonel Trunce was the C.O., and headed up the regiment of paratroopers that Joseph was assigned to. Colonel Trunce was already a combat veteran of World War Two and Korea, and had been in country in Vietnam from the beginning of US involvement.

As a young lieutenant, Joseph made the wise decision of listening to his non-commissioned officers and the other members of his platoon who had combat experience. They knew right away that he came from a background much like their own. He worked with the men as a team and soon they came to trust him and respect his courage. Joseph saved many of their lives more than once and they came to follow his command without question. He protected his men and accomplished his missions. Joseph soon became a Captain and carried on his leadership style. His colonel soon took notice and drew Joseph into his circle of confidence, trusting his judgment and his intellect. Joseph was never a 'yes man' and would put his two cents in regardless. If he disagreed with the orders he didn't complain, he followed them.

John Trunce was a soldier's soldier and, contrary to higher command directives, fought alongside his men whenever he was able. Colonels weren't supposed to be in combat with their troops: they were too valuable to lose. That's how it happened, that John Trunce and Joseph ended up behind enemy lines for two weeks on their own. They lived on grubs, mined from under fallen logs, and learned which ones tasted the best. They killed the enemy, and brought the war to the Viet Cong. They were cautious, disappearing like smoke after each stealth attack. They learned by doing and became experts at jungle warfare, and because they were fast learners, they stayed alive for those two hellish weeks. John Trunce had been trained by both the South Vietnamese and by Japanese Veterans of WW II. He was a jungle fighter of the highest skill and Joseph trusted him completely. Each developed a sense for what the other man was thinking and knew what he would do or not do. When they were finally able to cross back over enemy lines and rejoin their troops, John Trunce made sure Joseph became a major and was at his right hand. Joseph couldn't leave his colonel and did three tours of duty with him. When John Trunce went stateside, he took his major with him all the way to Patience County. It was as good a place as any. Joseph went to graduate school in St. Louis and earned a PhD. while John Trunce trained troops at Fort Leonard Wood, Missouri and went about the life of a career regular army soldier. John had long been eligible for retirement, and when his wife Kathy finally put her foot down, he left the military. John supplemented his pension as a consultant to defense contractors and trained troops for friendly foreign governments. John developed many military ties throughout the world in those years.

Joseph completed his PhD. In Botany and went to Africa to do field study in Kenya among the Masai people. Joseph had thought that being black would be enough to fit in. While it didn't seem to hurt, it became clear to him that he was treated as an outsider simply because he wasn't a member of the tribe. The Masai were fierce warriors and had never been conquered. Throughout history, the area's European and British invaders wisely went around the warrior nation.

As a botanist, Joseph worked with the local farmers, established irrigation, and did research. He loved working and living in such a different and challenging environment. His research facility was near the Masai camp where the local chief and his enormous extended family lived. Joseph picked up the language fairly rapidly, as the farmers who were important to his work spoke both Swahili and some English. Soon Joseph began to attend ceremonies and celebrations at the Masai camp and was treated as an honored guest. On one of these occasions, Joseph walked into camp and saw the most beautiful woman he had ever seen walk past him, accompanied by a large teenage boy, oddly holding her hand. Joseph thought it must be a Masai custom, or maybe just a show of affection. Not being stupid, he didn't go to the first warrior and ask him who the woman was. He didn't want to start an incident or be stabbed with a seven foot spear. He came to find out that the woman's name was Ua. She was one of the chief's daughters and had recently lost her husband to disease. The chief became increasingly aware of Joseph's efforts to help his people and decided that he needed an interpreter to learn more Swahili and the tribe's customs and traditions. To Joseph's eternal joy the chief gave that task to the same beautiful woman he'd seen in camp. Around the same time, the chief became more and more comfortable with Joseph. He began to send young women over to Joseph's tent when he stayed in camp. Joseph firmly sent them away, explaining that in his country, the girls were too young and that men and women had a courtship and marriage. The Masai understood the courtship and marriage part, but only if the woman was to be your wife. The chief thought Joseph a little odd to turn away these fine young women, but understood at least that all people are not the same, especially when they are not Masai.

Joseph and Ua worked together with the farmers and the people of the village. With her help his Swahili became better as did her English. They spent many long hours together and a friendship developed. Joseph spoke to her of the world, of the great warrior John Trunce and of America. She taught him the traditions of the Masai, their oral history, and all she knew of the local vegetation and its medicinal properties.

One day Ua introduced her son to Joseph. He thought it was a little bit odd that the boy seemed very childlike. He watched the boy chase and play with children who were ten or so. The kid had to be at least eighteen, he thought. He was almost six feet tall and weighed two hundred and thirty pounds. Joseph asked one of the villagers how old the child was and was told he had been born ten seasons ago. Joseph thought that he must have heard wrong, so he asked someone else and got the same response. Knowing that there had to be a mistake, he asked a local missionary if the Masai measured years differently. The response was no, ten seasons means ten years old. Ten years old, that's impossible! The kid could play professional football and probably give me a run for my money in a wrestling match, he thought, bewildered. Joseph gently asked Ua about the child and she said ten seasons, as if it was completely normal.

Joseph came to find out that the Masai, while they are certainly tall people, can also be big and heavily muscled, depending on their family history. It happened from time to time that someone like Ua's son was simply a giant. When American's think of history it goes back a couple of hundred years. For the Masai, it goes back for thousands of years. So when a giant is born, others have been in the past. And it is no big deal. Everyone has their role. The boy would just be a big warrior and herdsman, and that was good for the tribe. Once Joseph understood, he knew how to relate to the child. Joseph had numerous younger sisters and brothers, cousins, nephews, nieces. A huge extended family, all of whom grew up with very little more than the Masai seemed to need. They raised their own food and built their own homes. Joseph played with the boy, taught him things and soon he and Joseph became inseparable. It was clear to the chief that Joseph was in love with Ua and her son. The chief called Joseph and Ua to him and explained to Joseph that he could not have Ua as a union would be against tribal law. Later, after many tears, Ua told him that she too loved him but must obey the will of her father and their laws and she needed to look after the safety of her son until he reached manhood. Joseph pleaded his case with the chief but to no avail. He gave no explanation and was absolute in his denial.

Joseph refused to give up, and when his grant money gave out and he was scheduled to return to the U.S., he sent in his completed papers, his instruments, and asked the chief if he could remain with the tribe. The chief granted him the right to do so as a visitor, but he was to remember that he was not Masai. Now Joseph was really confused. He was permitted to stay as long as he liked, but could not wed Ua. Her explanation was it was the will of her father and therefore tribal law. Joseph continued to help feed the people, helped at the mission school, and spent as much time with Ua and the boy as possible. One full year went by, and once a month like clockwork Joseph would plead with the chief again to marry Ua. It was as if the guy was made of stone. He clearly hadn't offended the chief, who seemed friendly towards him in all other instances except the marriage refusal. Joseph didn't know what to do, but he was stubborn and refused to give up. Short of being born again into the Masai tribe, he just couldn't see a way other than to stick it out. At least he could be close to her.

It was well into his second year with the Masai that Joseph was awoken in the middle of the night by the roar of a lion. It was close and in camp. Joseph had seen many lions in Africa, happily from a distance. Every so often a lion was killed by the men defending their livestock, brought into camp, and displayed.

Hardened by combat, Joseph could go from sleep to action immediately. He was out of his tent before anyone else. He looked around and saw the unthinkable: Ua was within twenty feet of the lion, having been in the wrong place at the wrong time. The lion seemed ready to spring, and when it did Ua screamed and the lion flew through the air toward her. Just as he saw the lion prepare to jump, Joseph started to run; he'd never make it. He ran like the All-American he was; nothing could catch him. Many Masai came out of their shelters and ran towards Ua. They were left behind as Joseph ran past them and out of his shoes. Just when he thought he'd never make it in time, Joseph saw a miracle. Ua's son ran from behind his mother with a spear and managed to deflect the lion as it jumped. However, he did little damage. The lion turned on the boy and cruelly swiped the front of his body with its claws, tossing him aside. As the lion went in for the kill, Joseph ran into it broadside, and the cat and Joseph went down in a tangle. Joseph pulled out his combat knife and ran the blade into the belly of the cat, ripping up towards the heart. He stabbed and stabbed until the cat was still. Joseph knew how to make sure an animal was dead; he had learned on his fellow man. When he stood he looked over at Ua holding her boy in her arms. They both came to him at once and hugged and kissed him, more afraid for him than for themselves. The rest of the Masai who saw what happened began to cheer and to jump up and down. A huge roar went up from the people, and was repeated again and again. The chief had seen the whole thing and was celebrating with his people. Joseph was covered head to toe in the blood of the lion. The people came over and embraced him, covering themselves in blood as well. Joseph just stood there with the woman and child he loved clinging to him, sobbing with joy, his mouth hanging wide open. He had seen some things in his life, but this was just incomprehensible. During all of this the chief bounded over and embraced the three jumping up and down, shouting "you marry, you marry." After all of the times that Joseph had asked for Ua's hand the chief had flatly refused. His jaw dropped even further.

The next day, after the child's wounds had been treated and Joseph slipped him some antibiotics, the chief came to Joseph's tent and spoke to him. "Big marry, big marry," he kept saying, smiling like a madman. Joseph thanked him in Swahili and walked out into the camp to find Ua. Everyone he saw hugged and kissed him, including the warriors who gave him spears and shields. Every time he turned around he was given feathers and trinkets and eating bowls, all of the highly prized possessions of the people. He just couldn't figure it out. While Ua stayed with the boy he went to talk to the French Missionary, to find out what had changed.

"Well, you killed a lion with a knife. You now deserve to be Masai in the eyes of the chief," said the old missionary gentleman from Marseilles.

"What does that mean?" Joseph asked, unbelieving.

"It means that you can marry the girl and her son," the old man said smiling.

"You mean all I had to do was kill a lion and I could have married Ua?" Joseph shouted.

"Well killing a lion will pretty much do it in the eyes of the tribe. Very few warriors do it single handedly."

"If I had known that I would have killed one with my bare hands!"

"The Lord works in mysterious ways!"

"Hallelujah," Joseph laughed.

The marriage was indeed big, and eventually it became time for Ua, Joseph, and the boy to go back to meet the great warrior John Trunce and see Joseph's land. Within the span of one day, after all of their travel documents had been obtained, Joseph, Ua, and Nathan, as they decided to give him an English name along with his Masai name, were standing on John Trunce's porch, Joseph in the firm embrace of his colonel. The old dog even shed a tear.

CHAPTER
FOUR

Sunday came and Sam was able to walk through the woods to his parents' house. He got started early so he could meander a little bit along the way. There were several places along the trail to lolly gag and swim if he wanted. Immediately behind Sam's home a hill went up for another half mile or so before cresting a ridge and starting down into a pocket valley that Turner's creek ran through. It was all on family land and unspoiled. There had never been any development and it was an old growth forest. Sam was on a well-traveled trail that hooked up with trails all over the county.

The morning was already sultry and was promising to turn into another scorcher, but it was somewhat cooler under the oaks and maples and was even more pleasant as Sam made his way down towards the creek. The creek was fed by both a spring and runoff back in the hills several miles away. Sam had been to the source many times. It was a deep blue pool that seemed to originate out of a sheer rock face that was a couple hundred feet straight up. It was part of a state park where visitors were monitored for packing up their trash and told not to swim in the spring. The one time Sam and Nathan did they found out the water was extremely cold right at the source, which seemed to deter all but the hardiest of swimmers. Farther down on to "family land" the creek took many bends and curves, and there were many spots quite deep enough for swimming, diving, and fishing. Sam and Nathan had swum in these holes countless times and camped throughout. It was a place that a person could disappear into.

Sam took off his shoes and waded into the shallow edge of the creek. The water was cold enough to make his toes curl. He bent over and used his well-worn pocket knife to cut several large handfuls of watercress and slipped them into the wicker basket next to the mushrooms he'd gathered in the forest. He had learned his ability to forage off the land from his dad and Dr. Harper, and now that legacy would make a fine addition to the Sunday Potluck.

He finally came to a clearing at the edge of a meadow; about fifty yards down was Sam's parents' home. He could already see all the cars parked in the drive for the ritual of Sunday dinner. In the shade at the back of the house was a large stone patio with a built-in combination stone grill and wood-fired oven. The patio was dominated by a huge wooden table that was at least thirty feet long and built from enormous planks fastened together with construction bolts that were the biggest he'd ever seen. Seated around the table were his family and friends, as diverse a group as you'd find anywhere in the world. Foremost in the group was Nathan Harper, all seven and a half feet and five hundred pounds of him.

Nathan had just kept growing after he moved from Africa with his mother and father. Nathan looked every bit the African Prince. His skin was jet black and shown with a vitality and sheen that exuded good health. He was huge in every respect, from the spread of his massive shoulders and back to his huge but proportionate head. He had arms and legs as big as rolls of tar paper, his face proud and handsome. When Nathan saw Sam, he stood and embraced his friend as if he hadn't seen him in years, even though it had only been a couple of days. Sam and Nathan had grown up together from the age of twelve. Until Sam moved away, they'd spent every free moment with one another, fought at each other's side, learned about girls and the world together. When they were twelve years old, their fathers had started to train them in all of the physical Ranger skills, teaching them to shoot every manner of firearm, to fight with knives, to hide, to ambush, to track.

One summer, the four of them lived with the Masai and all learned the Masai skills. The Masai warriors and their chief were especially impressed with John Trunce. They could sense the true warrior in him. John was the first Trunce to become a Masai warrior. He simply stole away in the dead of night and returned the next morning with a dead lion, killed with a wooden spear hacked from a tree. Nobody asked for details and nobody questioned the kill. John had suffered some scrapes and bruises and a serious claw mark across his right leg for his trouble. The only person that he shared the secret with was Sam. John had set a spring trap for the lion with himself as bait. When the trap sprung and dragged the lion aloft, John rammed the spear into the lion's heart. He had done his lion anatomy homework and figured out where to stab the beast. He had practiced at home with a couple of wild boars. They weren't as big as the lion, but were probably meaner. Two summers later when Sam was in college he spent a second summer with Nathan and the Masai and tried the same trick, but the rope broke just as Sam stabbed the lion with a spear, missing the heart but significantly slowing the lion down. That lion stalked Sam through the veld and brush for hours. The battle was epic, and Sam had to utilize every hunting skill the Masai had taught him. Sam was dealt several glancing blows by the lion's claws and one deep one to his shoulder. The lion eventually couldn't climb and Sam waited him out for a full day and night. The lion eventually passed out and died from loss of blood. Everyone back at camp was concerned except for the Masai. Nathan had to restrain himself from going to look for his friend, but he knew that if anyone could kill a lion and get away with it, Sam could.

When Nathan had gone to kill his lion, his greatest trouble had been getting close enough to spear it, as lions are not stupid and any animal would flee from a five hundred pound man with a spear that looked like a flag pole. The Masai weapons makers had made Nathan several spears in his size. They looked a lot more like fence posts than spears, with the blade portion viciously long. Nathan practiced daily all of his life with his spears. It reminded him of his people and heritage.

Nathan never hunted with a gun, but loved to hunt and did so only for food. He learned from some of the good ol' boys in Patience how to hunt with a bow. He was deadly with a slingshot and could knock down birds in flight by throwing a rock. If Nathan had extra game he shared it with friends and neighbors. The very best kept secret about Nathan was that he excelled as a cook, learning at the town's restaurant by the river. While Sam goofed and flirted with young girls in the front, Nathan was back in the kitchen and garden learning cooking skills. He kept a large library of cook books that he constantly added to, and he studied many different styles. His produce and skill in harvesting wild foods were both legendary. Nathan was a man who stuck with the things that interested him and those were the things that he excelled at. He was concerned about what was happening in the world, but didn't diversify into many different pursuits. Nathan did most things by hand, except for plowing the larger fields. Most of his income came from the specialty produce he provided to fine restaurants across the county. He had established a profitable business doing so, often delivering his produce by UPS. He also raised ducks and geese and made his own goat cheese, all of which he sold in one form or another for great profit. He lived comfortably and frugally.

John Trunce also strode over and hugged Sam. He had never been the strong silent type, and had always expressed his love freely to his family and friends. It was probably John's love for the people who he cared for that made him such a fierce foe and warrior. When he fought for his country in foreign wars he saw not a faceless nation but his family and friends, and he fought for his men and his buddies. He had always been a front line soldier, had been wounded many times, had suffered diseases and was tough as nails. His combat experiences were with him every day but had never damaged him psychologically or changed his lust for life and experience.

"How's your wolf-dog, Dad?" Sam asked.

"I'm not sure if I'm keeping him or he's keeping me," John answered, smiling. "He sure keeps an eye on everything, me included."

Sam waved to Lisa Coleman, who was seated next to Nathan, along with John's mother, three of Sam's uncles. John's Vietnam buddies, Crockett and TJ were also there, along with a smattering of close friends and other relatives. One place was left empty for Tracy, Sam's older brother, who came once in a blue moon, when he was able.

The table was covered with side dishes and platters of fried chicken, catfish and beef roast. Dishes were passed back and forth while everyone talked at once.

"Sam, spook anything up in the woods on the way over?" Nathan asked piling chicken onto his plate.

"Hope you saw some more chickens," Crockett laughed, eyeing Nathan's growing pile.

"TJ, is my car done yet?" Sam's Uncle Bill shouted from the other end of the table.

"Just these mushrooms and greens for salad," Sam said adding his own words to the jumble of conversations.

"No bad guys, I hope," John added.

"No Dad, I think we ran all the meth makers and dealers out for good."

There were general murmurs of assent from all over the table. Everyone had pitched in to help Sam run the dealers out of town when he got back from Detroit. The drug war might be going on elsewhere in the nation, but Sam won the drug war in Patience County.

The Sunday Potluck continued until dark. When people finally started to wander home and to an early bed, Sam did the same, wondering what the new week would bring.

CHAPTER
FIVE

Virgil Ward looked out his window and said to his wife, "Them trucks keep driving up the old logging road. Did somebody buy that old saw mill up there, Martha?"

Martha paused with her hands in the dishwater, shook her head, and sighed. A man like Virgil should never retire. He was tolerable when he was at work. Now he was underfoot all the time.

"Virgil, leave it alone. If whoever owns the property has a problem with it I'm sure they'll complain."

Unfortunately, she couldn't think of any chore or errand that Virgil could do to occupy himself. The lawn looked like the greens at the Master's golf tournament. The car was cleaned and tuned like it could run at Indy. The garden was immaculate. Virgil was a perpetual motion machine. He'd been with the postal service his whole life. Now they only let him volunteer a few hours at the nursing home. He drove the residents to distraction.

When he first retired he would sit and stare at her in the kitchen telling her what to do. That lasted a couple of months until she took after him with a broom handle. He was shocked, but got the message. She loved her husband and he had always been a good provider, but she couldn't have him around all the time. It was just too tiring.

"I don't know, Marty, maybe I should call the Sheriff."

"Virgil, you do not need to bother Sam."

"Well, I'm going to do something about it."

"All you are going to do is to get yourself into trouble."

With that, Virgil walked out of the house and got into his farm truck and drove out of the yard.

About two miles over the hill from the Ward's, two men sat outside of an old storage shed, next to the broken down remains of an old band saw rusting in the sun. The younger one was in his early twenties, big and doughy, peering through greasy ribbons of stringy black hair that fell over his face like a curtain. "How long will it take Doc?" Greasy asked with a fidgety glance towards the shed.

"Shit boy, what do you want to do, lick the spoon?" the older man said. As he spoke he peered through wire rimmed glasses with heavily sedated eyes. Doc had been involved with illegal drugs for thirty years, with only marginal brushes with the law. This time around he was applying his chemistry skills to the manufacture of methamphetamine, a drug he himself would not use. He knew better from his old hippy days: 'meth is death.' It was a fantastic drug for creating slaves, just like Billy the drone next to him. Billy hadn't learned much since birth and what he did know was usually wrong.

Doc wasn't the origin of Billy's limitations. He was just a cook for an organization that was cashing in on the explosion of methamphetamine use in the rural Midwest. He was paid well, never participated in distribution, and didn't want to. He learned a long time ago not to ask questions and never to get bigger than the guy above him on the totem pole.

Billy pulled a cigarette from his shirt pocket and fired it up, hardly doing anything as a look out for their illegal operation.

Doc looked at Billy and felt a little bit sorry for him. He was a damn odd looking kid. He had an absent look about him, kind of goofy, compounded by the fact that he had a massively pronounced under bite; hence the unfortunate nickname of Bucket. Doc thought that when the kid had his mouth closed he looked almost like he was wearing the helmet of a suit of armor. Good Christ, I've seen it all now, he thought. It didn't help any that Billy, or Bucket, had been hitting the pipe hard enough that he had started picking at his face. He had dozens of angry pock marks. Doc knew that once a user got to this stage anything could be rattling around in his melon. Doc fingered the electric stun gadget in his pocket, wondering whether it would be of any use at all if Billy got feisty.

So far, it was still easy to get all the cold medicine that they needed to cook the methamphetamine locally. They even trucked it in from Mexico. As far as Doc knew, it might not be 100% legal to bring packing boxes stuffed with ephedrine tablets across the border, but the beef for capture was a lot less than for bringing in the finished product. The rest of the chemicals needed for cooking were available from most hardware stores or chemical supply companies.

Just as Doc was contemplating the process he saw an old man in a John Deere hat driving up the road in a pickup truck, plain as day.

"Now who the hell is this?" he muttered. Everything was going fine and now here comes the nosy neighbor.

"Billy, you let me do the talking. Don't do or say anything." It was hard to tell if Billy got any of that; his vacuous stare didn't reveal much in the way of recognition.

Doc stood up and walked over to the truck in a hurry to put the guy's mind at ease and get rid of him.

"Morning! Out for a drive?" Doc knew better than to rush these things. A nice neighborly chat usually did the trick. Doc tossed out his hand like a traveling salesman, Virgil didn't hesitate and returned the handshake, stepping out of his truck.

"Howdy, name's Virgil Ward, I'm your neighbor," Virgil said cordially, with a sideways glance at Billy.

"Oh don't mind him. He's my sister's kid. Slow you know." Doc gave Virgil his best conspiratorial look.

"I've got a few of them in my family too. You buy the old place then?"

"Well, we're in the process. We have permission to check the place out." The guy seemed to be buying it, Virgil thought.

Doc glanced over catching Billy meandering toward the shed where the last batch of meth was drying. Damn kid, now would be a nice time for the stun gun, bet the neighbor would love that, Doc thought ruefully.

"Billy, now you wait a minute, don't go in there," Doc pleaded noticing Virgil was walking over there too. Damn it. What did I do to deserve two idiots in the same day? He thought.

Just as Billy was opening the door, Virgil got close enough to smell the strong, solvent odor. He wrinkled his nose.

"Whoa, they must have left some chemicals in there."

"Yah, maybe you better not go in there." Too late, Virgil followed Billy into the building like a lemming and looked around. I might as well have told him, "Go right in."

Doc stepped into the shed and found Virgil standing smack dab in front of the work table where their beakers, tubes and hot plates were arranged.

"Well, what the hell is all this?"

Doc walked up to him and said, "I don't know," pulling the stun gun from his pocket and giving Virgil a zap. Down he went flopping like a fish tossed up on shore.

"Billy, goddamit! Look what you've done!"

No response, Billy was pawing in a pan of white powder drying over a large hot plate, completely oblivious. Doc marched over and gave Billy the full blast from the stun gun. That got a reaction, he actually turned his head. Oh no, Doc thought, that ain't good. Billy put some of the powder into a glass pipe, vaporized it, and sucked it into his lungs like a desperate vampire. His face twitched and jerked as he exhaled a giant plume of smoke.

"You just take a little," Doc said as Billy pawed around in the pan for another crystal. Christ, he doesn't even know what I just did to him. Doc shook his head. I've got to get somebody else on this job. He glanced down at Virgil and decided that step one was to tie him up. Doc grabbed a roll of duct tape from a shelf and bound Virgil's hands and feet and smoothed a piece over his mouth.

"Whenever you're ready, Billy," Doc said sarcastically. Apparently the drug had worked its way to Billy's brain, as there was a spark of recognition.

"Sure Doc," Billy mumbled as he ambled over and picked up a shovel.

Doc watched as the old man on the floor opened his eyes and started to make panicked noises through the tape.

"No Billy, damn it! Just put him in the back room and keep an eye on him."

Doc watched as Billy, the fucking wonder horse, grabbed Virgil by the ankle and dragged him off to a closet at the far end of the room. This was bad. Most people in the middle of nowhere leave their neighbors alone. Doc would now have to make a call he didn't want to make to his employer, the local representative of a particularly aggressive Mexican gang. Doc had been having his doubts about this particular operation; they'd saddled him with Billy, who liked the product too much, and chose a cooking shed too close to town for comfort. He didn't think the old guy's prospects were that good, though.

Doc sighed as he opened his cell phone and placed the call, "Its Doc. I need to speak to the Patron."

CHAPTER
SIX

Jose Carlos Menendez sat regally in the darkened room in a hotel in downtown St. Louis and held court. He was flanked by an odd assortment of men. Some white, some Hispanic, all trying their best to look tougher than the next guy. Menendez wasn't ruggedly good looking, handsome or particularly menacing in appearance. He styled himself as a boss or Patron, when in reality he was a nephew of the head of a Mexican Drug cartel safely back on the hacienda in Mexico. He was sent where it was thought he couldn't do much harm. His job was to make some meth, sell it and funnel the money back to Mexico. Regardless of his faults, he was loyal.

"Carlos, how are things in Patience County?" Jose asked.

"You got a call from Doc. Seems a neighbor got nosy and that idiot Billy went into the shed with the guy right behind him," Carlos sighed. He had been sent by Manny the Farmer to keep an eye on his nephew. This new development was just the latest result of a string of bad decisions Jose had made.

"Kill him."

"Which one?" Carlos said.

When there wasn't an immediate response, Carlos had to restrain himself from just taking the idiot over to the window and chucking him out. Any self-respecting St. Louis cop would take one look at the Tony Montana wannabe, bag him, and go for coffee. Who am I to say? Carlos thought. It would be like killing a blind dog anyway. He chuckled to himself and looked over at the mutt Jose kept with him at all times. Dogs do resemble their masters and this pair did in spades. Carlos remembered the ad that Jose had answered in the paper for well-bred hunting dogs. He and Jose had gone to the farm where the man was selling these 'rare' hunting machines. Carlos knew enough about dogs to know they were just straight coon hounds, nothing but legs, stomachs and howls. But he chose not to enlighten his 'Patron' on that occasion and figured Jose would board the dog somewhere anyway. Nope, the idiot kept his 'Lion', as he had named him, at his side day and night. The animal was without question the stupidest dog known to man. Lion would lie around like a wet rag and then suddenly for no apparent reason bark and howl like he'd treed a coon or sensed some invisible intruder. Jose would invariably haul out his gun and wave it around like something was going to get shot. After several discharges and a couple of hotel moves, with ample bribes to hotel managers, Carlos thought if there was any justice in the world, Jose would shoot the king of the jungle and Carlos could bury him in a dumpster. Carlos was the first to admit he wasn't much of a dog man.

As if on cue, following his master's outburst, the dog went into an absolute spasm. It was clearly evidence that animals could be possessed. The dog ran around the room, bit one of the soldiers and held on for dear life. It wasn't until Carlos tossed the remnants of a sandwich on the floor that peace was restored.

"Patron, perhaps Lion needs the open country to satisfy his great skill at hunting."

"Nonsense, I need him by my side and perhaps he will be a useful tool. I have taught him to 'sic balls'. He will attack any enemy I choose. We are a team."

Way too many gangster movies, sic balls my ass. Carlos wisely kept that thought to himself. That demented, inbred antelope might sniff balls or lick balls, but to teach him to regularly bite any specific target was unlikely.

Lion, having finished the sandwich flopped down, looking satisfied to resume his usual activity of sleeping, punctuated by growling and farting.

Hopefully the dog is dreaming of being eaten by a real lion, Carlos considered.

"I think it best if we don't leave a trail of bodies. We can just find another location and release the neighbor in a day or so. I can't imagine an all-out manhunt over a couple of days, so we'll just move the operation. There's so much nothing in that county that nobody will find us anyway. We'll give him a good knock on the head and set him loose," Carlos suggested.

Jose looked at him with a well-practiced Clint Eastwood squint, like he didn't believe what he was being told or was considering it. Instead he was just trying to understand it.

"He has seen."

"Patron, all he has seen is an old hippie and Billy the local junky who looks like a giant rain gauge. We'll move those two somewhere else."

"I will think on it," Jose said, dismissing the matter from further conversation.

As long as he doesn't discuss it with the other half of the 'team', Carlos thought.

Carlos picked up the cell phone and got Doc on the line, "Hold onto the guy, finish as many runs as you can, and call back in two days. We'll knock him out, pour a little whiskey down his throat and dump him in his car in the next county with a little roofie cocktail."

"Good call, boss."

"Keep an eye on Billy, I wouldn't trust him to hold a lantern in my front yard, but he has his uses," Carlos said not entirely sure of himself.

Doc turned the phone off and collected the finished product already made. He put enough to keep Billy cognizant into a smaller baggy and hid the rest under a floor board when the boy wonder wasn't looking. Doc thought the plan for Nosy was a good one. He'd start administering the Rohypnol when he gave the old guy a drink. He wouldn't remember anything, with a little whiskey on his clothes, a little dirt liberally applied and a condom wrapper in his pocket. No, he'd never say a word.

Virgil lay in the closet, his mind racing with numerous explanations for his predicament. Unfortunately, none of them even close to accurate. True to his nature, Virgil started at panic and worked his way down from there. Terrorist bomb making was his first choice, although he couldn't quite figure out what terrorist group would include an old hippie looking guy and that retarded freak. As he was contemplating that, Doc opened the door and pulled off his duct tape gag.

"I won't tell anyone about the bombs," Virgil blurted out as soon as he could get his sticky lips apart.

"Bombs?" Doc said looking at Virgil, thinking No way, nobody is that naïve. He instantly hit upon a plan. He could use the guy, but that meant he'd have to keep track of two loose cannons. Let's see where this goes, Doc thought making up his mind.

"Not bombs, secret work for the US government," Doc said trying to sound mysterious and spy-like. What the hell? He thought. Sometimes people want to believe so bad they'll buy anything.

"You must be undercover then," Virgil jumped in with both feet, seeing a ray of hope.

"Deep, deep undercover. I'm a government agent, code named Orange."

"I'm a good American; I can keep my mouth shut."

Doc smiled and started warming up to the whole idea. Billy won't have to kill the ninny and he might be useful.

"You military?" Doc fished.

"Army."

"I could smell it on you. Any combat?"

"Cook, they wouldn't let us fight."

"Best damn soldiers in the army."

"That's what I always said."

"I let you go soldier, and you're under my command. Could be days, could be weeks with no outside contact."

"What about my wife?"

"What about her? She's no combatant."

Virgil jumped right on that and said, "You're right, I wouldn't want to put her in harm's way."

She could probably use the lunatic vacation. It must be annoying to have a brainiac like Virgil underfoot all day. With that thought Doc cut through Virgil's tape with a box cutter and helped him to his feet.

"Now, it's best not to talk to Agent Bucket. He's like a coiled spring, lost his family to the enemy you know," Doc said jerking his thumb in Billy's direction.

"The enemy?"

"Japs, Chinks, Ruskis, Gooks, Arabs,"

Doc noted that Ruskis seemed to engender the most recognition.

"Yah, them damn Ruskis. But I thought they weren't commies anymore." Oh-oh! A glint of knowledge.

"All one damn hoax to get our guard down, soldier!"

"Knew it! Knew it! Told the wife, but would she listen? No, said I was an idiot, a nut job!"

"All straight from the top, the damn top!" Doc yelled.

Virgil couldn't help it. He sprang to attention and yelled, "Sir, yes sir!"

Doc wanted desperately to say, "Don't call me sir, I work for a living!", but he figured rank had its privileges and didn't feel like a self-inflicted demotion.

CHAPTER
SEVEN

Nathan Harper squatted silently in the bushes next to his enormous garden and waited. Somebody was stealing vegetables and needed to be caught. He shifted his weight and sat down, alternately peeking into the garden and sharpening his spear. Nathan generally had a sunny disposition but also a seriously demented streak. Sam could swear to that. He was looking forward to scaring the absolute crap out of whomever he caught helping themselves in his garden. His Masai shield and brightly colored clothing would get their attention. He wasn't going to hurt them, just have a little sport. When he was done, nobody would venture into his garden again without permission.

As Nathan considered the coming entertainment, he noticed a small movement at the edge of the woods and peered out with a wicked grin on his face. Nathan moved like a wraith through the brush and positioned himself to charge out. Bingo! A second later he was all pumping arms and sprinting feet, screaming at the absolute top of his lungs and waving his spear at the unfortunate trespasser.

Jimmy Dent peeked out into the big garden. He felt bad about taking vegetables, but he had a bunch of brothers and sisters, mom lived on food stamps, and dad was gone. He looked all around and finally crept forward on his torn up Chuck Taylors. He had a sack to stuff things into and moved out of the protection of the woods.

"Shiiiit!" Jimmy screamed when he saw the entire Masai nation charging down on him, eyes wild with rage, roaring over the sound of a giant spear crashing against a shield.

"Kill!" Nathan screamed until he saw it was some kid. In one motion he grabbed the boy by the waist and threw him into the pond right next to the garden.

"Don't kill me, don't kill me!"

Nathan was trying to remain fierce but the kid's expression had been too funny. He was laughing and shaking all over. The boy mistook it for a fit and started his own screaming again.

"Take it easy kid, I'm not going to hurt you," Nathan said, putting up his hand to calm the kid down as he continued to jiggle with laughter.

Jimmy was dumbstruck, not believing his eyes or ears. After a few uncertain moments, he started slowly swimming over to the side of the pond towards the biggest, blackest, craziest looking man he'd ever seen.

Nathan sat on the bank and the kid cautiously came out of the water. He noticed that even sitting down the man was taller than he was at twelve years old.

"So you're the potato thief. What the hell for?" Nathan looked the kid over and, seeing the state of his clothes and his skinny frame, decided he wasn't enemy number one.

"I took 'em home for my mom, she thinks people are giving them to me."

"You could ask, you know," Nathan said in a calming matter of fact way. He liked the boy right away. There was pride inside that lanky kid.

The kid couldn't take it anymore. "How tall are you mister?

"Tall enough that you should be smart enough to steal from somebody else. What's your name anyway?"

"I'm Jimmy Dent, you a real African warrior?"

That did it! The kid could think!

"Masai," Nathan said, striking his spear against his shield.

"What are you going to do to me?" Jimmy said directly, thinking he was going to get in trouble.

"Well, I was thinking you could work off some vegetables now and then. There's always something to do around a farm and garden."

"You have a deal."

"Then let's get you a real sack and some good potatoes and something to eat."

Nathan led the kid through a high hawthorn hedge twisted together, making an imposing barrier. "That's the Kraal, it keeps out the Lions." Nathan liked his kraal and its gesture to his Masai tradition. He and his parents had constructed it. In Africa, it was designed to keep predators out and provide an extra layer of safety for the people and animals inside. Here, it was more about tradition and making a home.

Nathan noticed that the kid accepted the notion that there were lions in the woods in stride. Perhaps he thought Nathan had let a few of them go out there. The kid was still a kid; he hadn't turned cynical or smart-assed yet. Maybe he wouldn't; they didn't always. Nathan thought of his buddy Sam. When they were young they were the model of manners on the outside, but sneaky and clever on the inside. You had to be that way with John Trunce around. You just didn't want to disappoint him, and you sure as hell didn't want to make him mad.

The two walked into a cavernous kitchen at the far end of which was a large steel door. Nathan said, "I know you like meat, all young warriors like meat."

"I like everything."

"OK! Then let's eat big!"

Nathan opened the door and walked into a large walk-in cooler. Sides of beef were hanging and there was farm produce everywhere.

"How about steak?" Nathan said. The kid just nodded and smiled. Nathan loved to cook for people his way.

With one hand Nathan grabbed an entire side of beef and lifted it off the hook so that it dangled from the ceiling. He dropped it to his side and carried it out of the cooler like a suitcase. The kid backed out, eyes like dinner plates. Nathan carried the beef over to a huge metal table in the middle of the kitchen, took a butcher knife out of a drawer in the side and cut long strips of meat along the back and loin area with swift, sure strokes. He left a fair amount of fat on the strips. The idea of a diet or limiting your food intake wouldn't even register to a Masai. Nathan cut what looked to the kid like enough for a family reunion and piled them on the table. He picked up the carcass, stuck it back into the cooler and pushed the slabs of steak onto a wooden board. By now the kid was following him around. Nathan went out back onto the deck where a good sized fire was burning in an opening in the deck. Nathan kicked the fire flat and threw some of the pieces of meat directly onto the coals, where they started to sizzle and sputter immediately. The kid and Nathan sat down and watched the meat cook. Nathan reached into the fire and turned the meat around now and then, pulling finished pieces out and handing them to the kid, who tossed them from hand to hand until he could hold them and then, just like Nathan, bite big juicy pieces out of the meat and chew them down. The kid ate like a champion and Nathan ate with a smacking joyful gusto. When all the meat was gone, Nathan led the kid over to a rain barrel where he dipped out a big pan of water that they washed their hands in.

"Time to garden, we're gonna pick peas." Nathan handed the kid a pail, took one for himself and advanced on the huge row of peas, trained up a long chicken wire fence. They worked their way along the row.

"You hunt and fish Jimmy?" Nathan asked dropping a handful of peas into his pail.

"A little, I mostly fish. I don't have a gun."

"You don't need a gun, Jimmy. I never use one to hunt."

"You throw that big spear at them?" Jimmy said clearly impressed.

"Sometimes I just throw a rock," Nathan said.

"No way!"

"I'll take you with me, you'll see."

The fierce Missouri sun was up and it beat down on the huge coal black giant and the brown as a berry boy as they filled up their pails happy to be in their element, outside.

CHAPTER
EIGHT

"It's time to move the operation, men." Doc circled his two 'men' with his hands clasped behind his back, really getting into the role. "We'll break camp, and then make a supply run for testing product!"

"Sir, yes sir!" both the old man and the sideshow kid yelled, one because he wanted to believe, the other because he was so sideways on meth and some other pills Doc had given him. Doc was pleased. Now he could send the old man into a bunch of stores in the area and buy up some cold medicine and other ephedrine products. Nobody would look twice at an old duffer getting cold supplies. All he needed was a cover plan that fit into the Russian conspiracy theory. And then, almost magically, it came to him.

"Trooper, it's all about mind control isn't it? Do you know how your government thinks those commie bastards are getting their mind control potions into Americans? over the counter medication. We've received orders to sample and test large numbers of these products from stores everywhere!"

"Now, where to start?" Doc looked at Virgil with a clear, 'what do you think?' sort of look.

"There are lots sir; it'll be like looking for a needle in a haystack," Virgil said.

"We're talking volume soldier. The Ruskies ain't gonna wait forever. How?" he snapped.

Bucket was no help. He was mastering the drooling catatonic pose admirably. Little more than a violent jerk of his head now and then indicated that he was an animate object after all.

"When people get sick, what's wrong with them?" Doc was trying not to suggest too much. He really wanted this to be Virgil's contribution to the mission.

"Well, sometimes they get a headache," Virgil haltingly suggested.

"What causes these headaches?" Doc was starting to feel like a game show host where the answers were incredibly easy and the host all but told them to the contestant.

"Bump on the head?" Virgil said with a little more conviction.

Doc had to bite his tongue. The clod, he thought. I'll give him a bump on the head. This guy's like a circus clown on ether.

"Yeeess....what else?"

"Maybe they run a temperature."

"Ahah"...light at the end of the tunnel. "Hot or...?"

"Cold?" Virgil guessed.

"Brilliant! You've got it! Cold medicine."

To his credit, Virgil shifted to the immediate acknowledgment that it was his idea. People are like damn sheep, Doc thought. And I'm the shepherd. The day was looking up.

CHAPTER
NINE

Sam put his feet up on his office desk hoping for a slow day as his phone rang.

"Sheriff, this is Martha Ward."

Sam punched the speaker function on his phone and answered, "What can I do for you today?" He knew Martha, and aside from the fact she had to whack Virgil on the head from time to time she was fine, and she saved Sam from having to whack Virgil on the head.

"It's Virgil. He didn't come home last night and I'm concerned."

"Any frying pan activity, Martha?" This was Sam's roundabout way of asking, "Did you clonk old nut butter on the head for a stupidity infraction?" Sam often thought the entire criminal code except perhaps for premeditated murder, could be summed up into three crimes: petty stupidity, plain stupidity, and gross-stupidity.

"Oh, of course not Sheriff."

"Just checking, Martha."

"Could you have the deputies keep an eye out? I'd appreciate it."

"I'll look into it myself. I'm sure there's a good explanation, Martha," Sam said, thinking if there isn't, Virgil better cook one up or stay away long enough so that she really does miss him. It didn't sound like a crime wave but Virgil was a homebody and could be laying in a ditch somewhere. Sam walked to the front of the station and called out to Lisa. "Virgil Ward is AWOL. Tell Swanny and Meyer to keep a look out for him too, will you? It's too soon for a missing person's report or a Patience County manhunt," Sam added.

Lisa waived her response, without looking up from the accounts ledger she was working on.

Sam walked out the front door and hopped into the squad just in time to see an out of state plate blow through the thirty mile per hour zone at better than sixty. Sam fired up the squad, heads turned, birds flew, animals took cover, and he was off. Sam followed the car until he could get a look at the guy inside: suit, tie, sunglasses, sneer, and he was driving a BMW. That alone was enough of an infraction for Sam. The idiot didn't even see him in his rear view mirror. Sam reached into his glove box, took out a pair of mirrored sunglasses and put them on. He pulled right up behind the dude and finally got a look back. Sam then pulled up alongside, never looking at the guy or turning on his lights. The driver looked straight ahead with both hands on the wheel, like a good old law abiding Joe. Sam pulled in front of the guy and started the old slow down maneuver. Just when they got down to thirty, Sam sped up and roared down the highway. Finally slowing to subsonic, Sam pulled over, screeched to a halt, and ran over to a smashed dead crow laying in the road. He kicked it into a plastic shopping bag and jumped back into the squad just as the other driver sped past. "The dumb ass," Sam said out loud as he fired up in pursuit. This time Sam pulled up on the right hand side of the preppy beamer man, made the universal "roll down your window" signal, and slowed them down so that the guy could hear him. Sam started to make some loud cawing noises and shouted, "Speeders in this county gotta adopt a crow!" He simultaneously flung the maggoty mess onto the guy's lap and slammed on his brakes. To his credit, business boy speeder kept it on the road with just a few sickening swerves as he crossed the county line.

Sam howled with laughter, knowing that in Patience all police complaints were directed to old Judge Holcomb, a dear friend of Sam and his dad. The judge just gave any complainers the statement, "no crime in Patience," and then the old hard-of-hearing, "Who? Who?" Who?" response to every question as if he was deaf. He liked to call it the 'owl' solution to alleged police misconduct. Sam thought that maybe the crow was a little much, and could have caused an accident, but if the guy had hit a kid in town, it wouldn't have been nearly enough. No ticket writing, and no way that guy would drive through Patience again.

After having been in Patience again for a few years after his big escape to the outside world, Sam had established his own informal contacts within the gossip community who he endearingly referred to as 'wildfire'. Finding out who was up to what and getting the subtle word out onto the street was as easy as one-stop-shopping. Sam's favorite contact was Jenny Turner, a local day care provider who, in addition to her talent for juggling toddlers, maintained what amounted to a central gossip clearing station. Someone was always dropping off or picking up and lingering to update or be updated. Sam eased the squad into traffic and headed over to Jenny's to see what she knew.

Sam really liked Jenny Turner, and shared a few misdeeds with her when they were growing up together all those years ago in town. She'd married a local boy, Steve Turner, who owned Shortie's Road House, on the edge of town, which had the best burger and coffee, and was where the locals got their money's worth when they ordered a mixed drink.

Sam pulled into the driveway and opened the gate that ran all the way around the property. He stepped through the gate and around several toys on his way up the sidewalk. Sam stepped into the doorway of the clean little building and was greeted by a commotion of squeals as several small children went scurrying across the floor, obviously in pursuit of something.

"Howdy, Sam. Be with you in a second, we've got a hamster escape," Jenny said from her position looking under an old brown sofa.

Sam carefully stepped over another low gate and into the play area, amused at the chaos, and scanned the floor. A little blond haired boy with a trickle of snot running down his nose looked up at him and pointed over into the corner, where a little golden hamster was chewing on the corner of a cardboard box.

"Dah," the child said, expecting Sam's immediate response.

As Sam looked at the kid he also caught a whiff of the kid's latest achievement in addition to hamster tracking. He remembered this kid as one of Jenny's handfuls. She must be feeding the kid spoonfuls of lead paint, he thought in a silly way. No way was he going to air that commentary; he just didn't know where crazy crap like that came from when it popped into his head. Since Sam's usual response to rodent issues was gunfire, he gestured to Jenny who swooped in and spirited the hamster back to his cage restoring order.

"Hey Jenny, I see you've got a houseful today. This one needs a change," Sam said waiving his hand in front of his face.

"His diapers are over there in that blue bag," Jenny said not entirely kidding. They'd known each other a long time. "What's up there lawman?" Jenny said.

"Virgil Ward's missing"

"I heard he's been gone from home going on his third day. It's pissing Martha off."

"Anybody see anything you know of?"

"Not yet," Jenny said deftly rangling the little blond boy down to change his diaper. "It seems a little weird, Sam. The guy's not bad in small doses. He's generally a homebody. A girlfriend is out of the question, unless she's as bad as he is."

"Two people like that together would blow up before any real relationship could get going. I'm going to poke around a little."

"From what I hear it's more like a lot lately," Jenny said with obvious glee. "I heard Jim Taylor's ex-wife brought over a pie and a six pack Saturday afternoon. Nice looking woman, especially in them short shorts."

"She was dropping an extra pie after the bake sale."

"My ass, Sam Trunce. What kind of pie?"

"Cherry."

They both laughed.

"I guess my life's an open book now that my girlfriend's gone."

"You can't burn a woman in effigy at a keg party and not expect some commentary."

"Now that was the Masai's doing. He's always setting stuff on fire."

"Oh sure it is, Constable. Blame Nathan," Jenny said finishing up the diaper and keeping a close eye on the children playing among the scattered toys on the living room floor.

"You going to give me more of that shit now, or bring it in a wagon later?" Sam said.

"I've got boatloads over at the bar. Come see us and tell Nathan I need some corn!"

"You are a bad woman Jenny Turner."

"I may be bad, but never boring," she said as Sam moved towards the door.

"By the way, what's the hamster's name?" He asked over his shoulder on the way out.

"Dah."

"Oh, of course," he muttered.

Sam made a few more stops, found that nobody had seen Virgil, and Sam started to worry a little himself. Missing people in a small community upset the natural balance of things. It was highly unlikely that Virgil was out on a bender. Sam knew most of the juicers locally from his own liquor establishment recon, as he called it. Virgil wasn't much of an outdoor guy and his car was gone. What the hell, nobody would grab him unless he saw something that he shouldn't have. Time to start from the beginning and earn my keep, he thought, and steered in the direction of the old mill next to Ward's. Sam turned up the road, stopped the squad next to the larger shed, and slid out of the car. He automatically pulled a side-by-side 12 gauge out of a holster attached to the back of his seat. He remembered all of the times he'd wished he could have carried a good old blunderbuss on some of those calls in Detroit. This one was a mean bastard and sounded like a cannon when it went off. Screw that keep-your-gun-holstered bull, nobody to worry about hitting here except possibly a bad guy, a rabbit, or a squirrel, all which were perpetually in season in Sam's book. Since he had narrowly escaped death when he'd been shot in Detroit he really didn't feel the need to yell "freeze" anymore. You know, war is hell. If the bad guys see a cop car and shoot anyway, their intention is quite clear.

Sam walked over to the shed and pushed the door open with the barrel of his shotgun. He walked in and noticed a lingering chemical smell and a pile of lye and solvent bottles. He went out a side door and over to a burn barrel. The barrel had seen plenty of use and the majority of its contents looked like gummy ash, wet with the recent rain. He stirred the contents around with a stick and saw a couple of cold tablet boxes that had survived. As he continued to walk around the area he found a lump of melted plastic pill cards, what looked like hundreds of them. The men that had been there recently might as well have left a sign announcing the presence of their former lab.

"So a cook comes to Patience," he muttered aloud. He must have overlooked the 'bad god damn idea' portion of the chamber of commerce literature. One lab usually meant more. It was time for a little scouting mission.

CHAPTER
TEN

Sam drove the squad over to his parent's farm and pulled onto the gravel drive way and followed it up to the modest farm house he'd grown up in. It was nothing fancy but was lovingly maintained, from the cedar siding to his mother's gardens spaced throughout the yard. Funny how the chores still seemed to get done, even though he and Tracy had moved out long ago, he thought. His father stood on the front porch talking to Nathan Harper. It never failed to amaze Sam to see Nathan standing next to any other human being; he just dwarfed everybody. But Sam and everyone in the know knew the old man was the far more dangerous of the two. John Trunce retired from the U.S. Army, a three war vet, a paratrooper and a ranger. He'd been a career soldier. When the old man's army buddies talked to Sam about his dad it was with an almost mystical reverence, with a strong 'do not piss him off' message. Sam was glad to have him on his side.

"Samson, come over and hug the old man." Nathan gave Sam a playful grin. Sam only allowed his father to call him Samson. The thought to ask him not to had crossed his mind, but his practical side told him that they'd be wasted words. Of course Nathan took the opportunity to call him Samson too. Sam smiled back with a 'that's going to cost you look'.

"Dad, Sideshow," Sam said bantering back.

"I feel great sorrow for you, Samson. Your wit diminishes with your age much like your attraction to women. I see it's more pity that motivates them now, whereas a great Masai warrior becomes more powerful and magnificent with age."

All three men laughed out loud.

"Hey, I've got a situation with Virgil Ward. He's AWOL." Sam said.

"And that's a problem?" John asked.

"Martha says he's been gone awhile now, a couple of days. I found some drug lab crap at the old saw mill where Martha said he went up to check on some cars going up there."

"Meth?" John asked his own anger building. "It can't be the same people as before. Nobody would come back after the welcome we gave them."

"Yah Dad, like before, but I don't think it's the same people. The remains of the lab that I just looked at seemed more organized. They burned their trash and tried not to leave much evidence. They must have left in a hurry. The place still stank of chemicals, but they didn't leave any empty chemical cans or other equipment. My guess is they know better than to attract attention. These are professional cooks. They won't be easy to spot."

"What's your plan?" Nathan said.

"I thought we could go up in your plane and look for Virgil's truck. We also need to see if we can spot any more active labs."

"Are you going to call in any outside help?" Nathan asked.

"I think gentle persuasion would be best."

"The usual subtle Trunce message?"

"Of course," Sam said.

"Fantastic, I get to blow something up," was the old soldier's beaming response.

"No crime in Patience," Sam responded.

An hour later, John was circling around the area in a restored P-47 Thunderbolt. The plane just roared. It was the kind of thing Zeus would fly around in if he needed transport. John loved the old Thunderbolt and called it the Angel. Of the few war stories that John shared with noncombatants was how during the Second World War, as a barely nineteen year old paratrooper, a lone Thunderbolt had impossibly come out of the sky and saved his company's collective ass. John had said that of all the times he'd faced death as a soldier, that time he'd just accepted it as given. Ever since that day, every problem in his life had been insignificant in comparison. John was not glorifying war; he hated it as most combat vets do, knowing it for what it is. Sam had seen some limited combat during his stint in the Special Forces, and was told how worried his father was when Sam had been sent into a combat zone. Sam also accidentally heard his father apologizing to his mother, finally understanding how it felt to be the loved one left behind when the person you love is off at war.

The old plane had a great roaring sound that carried for miles. John scanned the ground and radioed back to Sam.

"I don't see anything obvious yet," John said.

"The trees give too much cover. We'd better just concentrate on the clearings where we've got some old homesteads that aren't occupied," Sam observed.

"How much space do these maniacs need?"

"Not too much. It's more the smells, trash, and byproducts. You remember that strong chemical smell."

"I suppose when you make drugs with lye, solvents, and god knows what else someone nearby is gonna know it," Sam said.

A few hours went by and John noted a few places Sam wanted to check on a plat map. After a couple of barrel rolls and wing overs John landed. Sam was ready for a chair on Nathan's deck and some meat.

Sam drove out of the small airport where John and his buddy Cecil Tripoli stored their planes, and Tripoli kept things in order. Tripoli was another one of John's war buddies and had been a p-47 pilot in the waning days of WW2. He'd spent the rest of his career first as an airline pilot and eventually as an executive for a national airline. He'd taught John to fly, all the way up to some hours in a commercial jet, but both men liked planes with some teeth. Sam had never asked these men if the machine guns were operational. He didn't want to know. He did sneak a peek from time to time to see if there were any cartridge belts in the wings, but so far there were none.

Sam picked up his radio and called his office to tell the Lisa to contact the on-duty deputies and have them stop over at Nathan's for dinner at the end of their shift. Sam's plan was to cover possible meth lab sites John had seen from the air and to start asking around about old Virgil.

Sam rumbled onto the highway and saw a mini-van pulling a U- Haul off to the side of the road. There was a woman kneeling in front of a flat tire struggling with a tire iron. Always one more stop, Sam thought, intending to help get her back on the road. As he pulled in behind the trailer the woman stood and turned. A wild mane of curly jet black hair framed her dark eyes. As she stood, Sam could see that she was tall and athletically built, with a darker, almost gypsy-like complexion. Sam found himself transfixed in his seat, openly staring at the woman. Some little signal jarred him into action and he almost forgot to put the vehicle into park as he got out.

"Can I help?" He heard himself say.

"Je ne comprends pas," she said, pointing to the tire.

"You're French."

"Oui, je suis francaise."

Just as Sam's trance deepened, John drove up in time to hear the young woman speak.

"Comment ca va?" John said as he walked up.

The woman walked past Sam. His father and the woman immediately engaged in an in-depth discussion that absolutely flabbergasted Sam. This was without a doubt the most beautiful woman he had ever seen, and his father was speaking to her in fluent French. He didn't even know the old man could speak French that well.

"Don't just stand there boy, fix the tire." The old man smiled and made some off-hand comment to the woman and Sam got a glance and a smile from her that just made it worse. Sam looked down at his feet, picked up the jack, and addressed the tire. As he was getting started a small boy popped up in the back seat and stared down at him. Sam looked at the traffic on the road and saw that it was light and the car was far enough off the road. Besides, his bubble lights were on.

"Dad, ask her if her son can help me with the tire."

Sam heard another string of high speed French and the woman called to the boy. Sam had him step out and stand beside him, and walked him through the tire change. The boy said nothing but watched intently with intelligent and interested eyes. Sam loosened the lug nuts and then showed the boy how to loosen them. Sam and the boy worked together and soon the tire was changed. John and the woman were laughing and smiling and having a great time. He stood up and with the boy walked over to them.

"C'est mon fils, Samson," John said, gesturing to Sam.

"Samson?" the woman said, smiling and raising her arms up in a very intriguing double biceps pose. She was obviously a weight trainer, but her size was fluid and balanced.

"Thanks you mean old man," Sam said.

"And this is Christine," John said.

Just as John said that the woman leaned over and kissed Sam on both cheeks. Shocked, he murmured, "God love the French."

"Christine is Madeleine Toche's granddaughter," John said and immediately translated. "She's here to help with the restaurant."

Madeleine Toche ran Patience's only upscale restaurant. The food was uncomplicated but lovingly prepared. The flavors were bright and the ingredients fresh that day. It was just like a neighborhood restaurant that every little French town has. It was full every night with townspeople and visitors who had heard about Patience's secret.

"Let's show her the way to the restaurant then," Sam said, the tire fixed and the flat stowed in the trunk of his squad.

"A little French wine would be great," John said.

"Ah oui un peux du vin," Christine said smiling.

"She said..." John started to say.

"Got it Dad, she said wine and that's good enough for me."

Sam led the way about half a mile back into town to a larger looking house that Madeleine Toche had converted years ago into a quaint, serviceable restaurant, with a stream that rambled past it through a thicket of cottonwoods and oaks. As the little caravan pulled up, Madeleine Toche came out and walked over to greet her granddaughter. She was slight and petite and was ramrod straight, an absolute bundle of energy. She cooked and ran her restaurant with the help of three women from town. The menu was what she wrote on the chalk board and it was ready when you were. Sam had eaten meals there that had lasted hours. She was no nonsense and took her food, especially the ingredients, very seriously. Nathan Harper grew most of her produce and her meat came from the farms in the area. The trout was local, and when she felt like ocean fish she bought it fresh with a phone call to St. Louis, seasoned with the herbs she grew around the building.

Everyone followed Madeleine into the restaurant by way of the kitchen. It was immediately obvious to Sam that Christine more than knew her way around a kitchen by the way she looked at the equipment and the food that was underway. While Christine stayed in the kitchen the rest of the party walked into a small family dining area and sat around a large oak table.

"John, you know where the wine is," Madeleine said.

"Mon plaisir, Madeleine," he answered with a smile.

"Sam, your father is a rogue."

"He says that's why my mother married him."

"But of course. Why marry a boring man?"

John came back and set several ordinary glasses on the table and a large carafe along with a pitcher of well water. He poured wine for everyone including a little for the boy that he thinned with some water.

"How come I never got any wine as a kid?" Sam teased.

"You got plenty. I just didn't give it to you."

As they chatted for a while Sam kept glancing back towards the kitchen. Madeleine noticed and smiled.

"Christine won't come out of that kitchen for some time, Sam. She is a chef, a Cordon Bleu. She makes my humble country food seem ordinary."

"She's remarkably beautiful." Sam was beyond pretending disinterest.

"She has left her husband, also a chef in France. I think he couldn't stand it that she was a better chef than he. He gladly demonstrated that by sleeping with just about every young woman around." she said acidly.

"I thought being a rogue was good," Sam offered back.

"There is a difference between being a rogue and a pig." Madeleine's assessment of Christine's former husband was also a message that Sam picked up on immediately.

Sam made up his mind immediately. He stood up, laid his hand tenderly on Madeleine's shoulder and walked back to the kitchen without another word.

"You know Sam's a one woman man," John added.

"If I thought otherwise he would be busing tables."

"You could get him to do it too."

As Sam walked back to the kitchen he noticed a familiar sight out the window. Nathan had driven up on a large tractor with the seat modified to hold his huge frame. Nathan rarely used the tractor for anything except the heaviest farm work. Everything else from moving big rocks to clearing trees, he did by hand. It made him stronger than hell and gave him an enormous appetite.

"Oh no you don't," Sam muttered as he hurried through the kitchen and out the back door. "Stop right there you big African bastard."

"So, the granddaughter has caught the attention of 'he who entertains wayward women on Saturdays'," Nathan giggled.

"I saw her first. Besides you get enough anyway, so I guess I'd have to fight you for her," Sam said.

"I have seen pictures. Her beauty would drive you to great fierceness. How would you plan your attack?" Nathan said.

"I would hide up in a tree and drop down and hit you over the head with a log, "Sam said continuing the charade.

"That might work, but in the interest of saving my head and you the trouble of climbing a tree, I will be like a big brother to her."

"So when did you see pictures and why didn't you say anything?" Sam asked.

"She lived in France. I didn't know she was here until Madeleine called me. Now let's go in. I'm thirsty," Nathan said as he lifted up an earthenware jug cupped in his hand, unable to get his smallest finger through the handle.

"A delivery?" Sam said.

"Just some sugar and corn and stuff," Nathan smiled. Sam shook his head. Ever since Nathan first saw a still he had been mesmerized. Sam figured it reminded him of his childhood back in Africa, where the women brewed beer for the village.

As the two men walked back through the kitchen, Nathan said, "You're in trouble Sam. If you didn't notice she barely even glanced at me. I caught her looking at you when we walked on by."

"Man, I feel like a kid in school," Sam said.

"Lots of other hound dogs around here not as nice as me. Better not wait," Nathan said.

Sam was already back down the hall to the kitchen.

Things were picking up in the kitchen for the evening meal. Sam had eaten at the restaurant so many times throughout his lifetime that he recognized many of the dishes. There was often something new that Madeleine would present to her customers. Sam smelled lamb and looked over to see Christine adding some final seasoning to an earthenware pot of Daube, a Provencal heavy stew, one of Sam's favorites. One of the women was preparing some trout that would be fried in one of the heavy iron skillets heating up on the range.

Christine saw Sam walk into the kitchen and gave him a friendly, brief smile. She was in her own world like a captain at sea, with a finger on everything at once, like a conductor, melding the strings and woodwinds at just the perfect moment. The little boy had wandered into the kitchen and sat in the corner, watching his mother and keenly aware of what was going on.

"Yves, un peu du thyme, s'il vous plait."

The boy got up off the chair and motioned to Sam to follow him outside.

Sam followed and the boy and he walked over to a knee high planter just around the corner. The boy pointed to a thick patch of low shrubby thyme.

"C'est du thyme," the boy said, snapping off some twigs.

"Oh," Sam said, pretending not to recognize the plant. Everybody loves to show what they know. It was a nice moment and Sam didn't want to do the stupid adult thing and say, "yes, I know," or something equally pointless. Sam remembered showing both of his parents all of the herbs in these gardens when it was he that ran and picked for Madeleine.

Sam tried something else.

"Do you fish?"

The boy knew it was a question but shrugged his shoulders.

"Poisson?" Sam knew that from reading the menu over the years. He also made the universal casting and reeling of an invisible rod.

"Ah oui!" the boy said, very excited.

"We poisson," Sam said, pointing to the boy and himself.

The two of them walked back into the kitchen, the boy ran over to his mother with a small clutch of thyme, and with a rapid fire exchange the fishing date was decided.

Christine looked at Sam and pointed at the ground and said, "maintenant?" Her gesture suggested immediacy like, "right now?" Sam wished it meant "come over here so I can kiss you again." No such luck.

"Tomorrow morning."

"Au jour du matin," Madeleine said as she walked into the kitchen, settling everything with a wave of her hand as she put her arm around Sam and led him out of the kitchen. Score one for me, Sam thought, some fun with the kid and a chance to see mom again.

The next morning Sam got up, dressed, and went over to Nathan's to do a little work before they took the boy fishing for trout in the creek. He wanted to check a couple of the potential lab sites, and he hoped like hell that the cooks had moved on and they'd come up bust. Sam was not the kind of cop who wanted to find illegal activity, imagined or otherwise, as he had seen some nut cops do, the ones who wore the leather driving gloves and carried a giant side arm. Knowing how and when to shoot meant a lot more than having the blasting power. His father had told him that if rifles and machine guns don't do it, you'd better have armor. His father knew what he was talking about, having seen Tiger tanks rolling in his direction on more than one occasion in France.

Nathan was standing at the entrance to the Kraal when Sam drove up. He walked over to the car, carrying a spear the size of a large sapling, and strapped it to the top of the squad on two small rails that had been welded to the roof. He also had a holster attached to his side that held a short bar-reled shot gun, a 10 gauge side by side that had been modified so Nathan could get his finger on the trigger without discharging it.

"I see you brought the blunderbuss. Expecting trouble?" Sam smirked.

"Every time I am with you on one of these 'look sees' something hap-pens and a warrior never has empty hands," Nathan said as he wedged himself into the modified back seat. Even the squad groaned a little as he settled in. Sam had built in an extra heavy duty bench seat. It was more like a day bed. Nathan sat in the middle to balance the rig and off they went.

"The first stop is over near Taggert's ridge. There's an old trailer there and Dad thought it looked like there was some extra activity from the air."

"You're the sheriff Sammy; just tell me what to do."

"The usual," Sam said.

The usual was that Sam would go in and investigate while Nathan patrolled in the woods, acting as a lookout and back up so that Sam wouldn't be surprised from behind. Sam always brought Nathan. He knew that no matter what happened, Nathan would not leave him. The day that happened was the day Sam would quit believing in anything.

Sam and Nathan parked the squad off the road, down an overgrown cart path and out of sight. Without discussion Nathan disappeared into the darkness of the trees and was gone. Sam smiled when he thought of any poor bad guy stumbling upon the giant African prince in the woods, especially given Nathan's sense of humor. It was just wild how Nathan could blend into the woods so completely. Sam knew the Masai didn't fight or hunt in wooded terrain, but were especially adept at stealth in environments with very little cover. Given cover, Nathan said any child could do it. It was about knowing where your enemy was, not having to see him all of the time. Just like Sam's father and his boot camp drill instructor had told him. If you can see to shoot the enemy, he can see to shoot you. That's one of the undisputed truisms from the day of the bow and arrow.

As he carefully approached the trailer, Sam could tell that nobody was around. When he got near he purposely banged a couple of old rusty cans together and stayed under cover to see if anyone would flush. Nothing, Sam thought as he approached the trailer out of line of the windows and doors. He saw the telltale signs of manufacture activity. There were piles of solvent cans and lye containers. Sam proceeded with caution around to the back and peeked into a window. There were stacks of garbage and old fast food containers. The only occupant was a raccoon picking around. Satisfied, Sam cautiously went in the back door and looked around. He walked to the front and made a loud screeching bird like sound to call Nathan in. It was the only one he knew. He figured it sounded wild enough to sound natural, at least natural enough to fool your run-of-the-mill druggie.

Sam walked out front as Nathan ghosted up to the trailer.

"No sport today?" Nathan said.

"No, it's just an old meth lab. These guys are smart enough to keep on the move." A piece of paper ground into a tire track caught Sam's attention; he stooped over and picked it up.

"Sure as hell, Virgil Ward's gas credit card slip," Sam said shaking his head. "One way or another Virgil is with these guys."

"He's no criminal," Nathan said.

"Only if you considerer dumb ass a criminal offense. The only drug Virgil needs from time to time is a smack from a frying pan," Sam said as he tucked the receipt into his pocket. "How about we catch some fish with the kid, make some calls, and have a little get together. Don't forget to call your dad."

"I would never make that mistake. I would never hear the end of it."

"Old soldiers are like that," Sam said.

Sam and Nathan drove over to the restaurant where Yves and Madeleine were sitting on the front porch, cleaning green beans.

"Nathan, mon chou," Madeleine said.

Nathan smiled, "Hardly have to clean 'em, do you?"

"Beautiful as always," Madeleine said.

"We're here to take the boy fishing, Madeleine," Sam said.

"Good, Christine wants to go too."

Nathan started to giggle, gently singing a Masai betrothal song. Sam of course knew it. He'd spent two of the hottest summers of his life with Nathan's tribe, and the two were regular visitors. Sam loved the easy, live for-the-now atmosphere of tribal life. Everyone worked and shared. Sam often thought that communities used to be more like that in this country in a loose, neighbor-help-neighbor, barn raising sort of way.

"We'd love to take her fishing. She should wear some clothes to get dirty and a hat for the sun."

Madeleine smiled at Sam as if indulging a child's silly comment. "My family is from Provence. Your sun is quaint compared to Marseilles this time of year. We also know a little about fishing."

Just then Christine came out onto the porch. Sam straightened up despite himself. She had on a frayed cotton top and cutoff jeans, buttoned over a bikini bottom along with worn leather sandals.

"Sammy will spend a lot of time in the cold creek today," Nathan muttered.

Whoa, Sam thought. Christine was as beautiful in her beach bum outfit as any model he'd ever seen. Forget that 'elegant-as-a-sparrow crap', this woman's beauty was uncontrolled and savage. She was looking at him with true pleasure; it was palpable to everyone.

"We fish?" Yves said, used to men's reactions to his mother, taking Sam's hand.

"We fish," Sam said as he bent down and picked the kid up by his ankle and slung him over his shoulder. No need to translate that. Old Sammy's the fun one he thought, as the kid let out peals of joy.

They drove the squad over to Nathan's farm and parked next to a log shed where the fishing poles were kept. He grabbed some fly casting rods and a couple of beat up old cane poles.

"So we cheat today?" Nathan said as he picked up a pole. Nathan and Sam had spent so much time in the creeks of Patience growing up that they would generally creep up to special pools and eddies where the trout would hang and catch them by hand. They shined frogs that way too, never using a gaff. That way they could have the fun without killing the bullfrog. They both liked frog legs, but it was hard to kill a big ol bull frog. It wasn't about being squeamish, far from it. But most of the time a frog really does look like it's minding its own business. Particularly with all the old stories about the frog prince, lawn ornaments, kiddie frog pools, and frog floaties. The frog has some standing in the amphibian-man world. You can't just throw a spear through him, especially one that looks like a trident, so that the frog's last thought was, "eh tu Poseidon?"

"We'll show 'em both ways."

"Which one are you going to teach, my friend?" Nathan teased.

"We'll all go together there, Farmer Nate."

The sun filtered down through the tree tops and a gentle breeze made the temperature pleasant. The fresh smell and moisture in the air near the creek and the dark shadows cast from the banks kept the heat of the day away.

They walked, carrying the poles and a small tin can of grasshoppers across one of Nathan's pastures, ducking under some low lying branches and down a short hill to where the creek ambled by. As they walked over the whitish stones that were the creek bed when the water was higher, Sam saw a water moccasin and pointed it out to Yves and Christine. He demonstrated by curling two fingers over like fangs and striking his arm, "Ne touch pas," he said.

"So you do know some French. What's it mean?" Nathan said.

"It means don't touch."

"Obviously you've met a French girl before."

"Once or twice," Sam said with a grin.

The creek meandered under and around oaks and cottonwoods, twisting around with a few straightaways. The depth varied as the creek bit into the banks and created some deep pools and shady spots where Sam and Nathan always found something. It was cool and still under the canopy, with only a slight rustle of the cottonwood leaves at the very top of the trees. The sound of cicadas was everywhere. Sam reached up and cupped a cicada out of a tree and showed it to the boy. He was fascinated by the large, prehistoric looking insect and reached out to touch it right away.

"We'll turn him into a Missouri country boy yet, just like I did you," Sam said.

"No, I turned you into a Masai warrior who happens to live in Missouri."

Sam took a fly out of a small packet in his pocket and tied it to the end of his line and gestured for Yves to follow him to the edge of the water. Sam dropped the fly into the current and let it be carried down into a small pocket just adjacent to a patch of faster running water. Just as the fly floated into the pocket there was a silvery flash as a trout took it. Sam handed the pole to Yves and showed him how to pull back and land the fish. The boy landed a beautiful rainbow trout just the right size. Sam showed Yves the gunny sack to put the fish in. The kid was way ahead of him. He easily took the hook from the mouth of the fish, dropped it into the bag, tied the top with a cord, and set the bag into the stream, weighing it down with a rock. Yves then took the pole and promptly caught another fish. Just as that happened, Christine picked up one of the fly rods, attached a fly and expertly flicked it into another small, likely pool, almost immediately hooking into one.

"Who's teaching who, Sammy?" Nathan said, duly impressed.

"I bet they can't catch 'em in their hands," Sam answered.

"No way am I betting against ole Bill Dance there. She's as good as I've ever seen," Nathan said.

It was true. Christine handled the rod with complete control and touch. It was like watching her dance. She looked just like she belonged in that stream, casting for trout thousands of miles away from the Mediterranean under the Missouri sun.

CHAPTER
ELEVEN

Janice and Patty smoked cigarettes as they walked down the well-worn trail, oblivious both to the beauty of nature and the beer cans and cigarette butts that lay along the path, evidence of parties long past. They were two teenage friends, bonded by their mutual boredom and their willingness to try just about anything to get high.

"Hey, let me see that stuff again," Janice, the taller red haired teen, said.

"Just hold on. We're almost at the fire circle. Aren't you high enough? That last joint was crazy," Patty said, a little loopy eyed, giving her a friendly pat on the arm.

"I'm tired of weed. I want to try that new shit, supposed to be like cocaine," Janice said.

"You've never had any damn cocaine," Patty said.

"Yes, I did too, at that frat party we got into when we visited Mary's brother at State."

"It was probably a crushed up caffeine pill," Patty said.

"It worked on me."

"Everything works on you, especially frat boys." They both laughed and leaned on each other as they lurched up the path.

The girls walked into a clearing where some logs had been arranged around a fire pit that had seen some use.

"My mom used to come here and party years ago. I heard her talking about it to one of her friends," Janice said.

"So she knows you come here?" Patty said.

"Don't be stupid. No way. Parents don't want to know."

"Did she ever smoke dope or anything?" Patty asked.

"I doubt it; she was more part of the beer drinking crowd. She's still pretty straight that way. We don't talk about things like that. She's more worried about me getting pregnant and making decent grades than doing drugs. I think she knows we do some drinking, but nothing about weed," Janice said. "We smoke this stuff, right?"

"I've got a pipe I got from Henry," Patty said.

"Where did he get crystal meth?"

"That's like the last thing we need to know," Patty said.

"True."

Patty pulled a small glass tube and a folded tin foil packet out of her pocket. Both girls looked at it like they were examining an alien life form.

"How much do you put in?" Janice asked.

"He said just to put some in that little bowl and heat it up and inhale the fumes," Patty said.

"Go for it," Janice said.

Patty sparked a lighter, vaporized the grains of methamphetamine and inhaled.

"Whoa," she said as she blew out the smoke. "Holy shit!"

Janice had already taken the pipe and finished off the rest.

"That's awesome."

"No shit."

"Hey, give me one," Janice said as Patty lit up a cigarette.

"Man, now I know what everyone is talking about, this is outrageous."

"I don't see why everyone's so wild about this stuff. People just do it too much and get screwed over by it."

"Give me a little more."

Both girls took turns burning up the small amount that they'd been given as a sample. They smoked cigarettes and talked about their new discovery. They had instantly decided that the first order of business was to get some for the weekend and take it to a party. A friend of theirs was having a party to celebrate his parents being gone for a few days.

"Man, what time is it?" Patty asked.

"Like five."

"We got to go. I've got to be home before my mom gets there," Patty said.

"Alright, let's go."

"Make sure you keep it cool when you see your mom," Janice said.

"She doesn't know shit and we don't smell or nothing."

The girls made it back down the trail and to Patty's car. They got inside and pushed the hamburger wrappers aside and found a fresh pack of cigarettes. Patty cranked up the local rock station, and soon the whole car was vibrating to a blaring, rapid-fire beat. With the wind in their hair and the drugs making everything seem like so much fun, Patty drove faster along the park road, ignoring the speed limit and the upcoming stop sign.

Just as the girls turned off the tar leading from the state park, a ranger truck rounded the corner off the gravel. Patty blew through the stop sign and into the path of the ranger truck. The impact knocked the girl's car onto its side.

"Where'd they come from?" Mike Schmidt blurted out to his fellow conservation officer Charlie Berry, as their car came to a jolting stop, throwing them both against their seat belts.

The two jumped from their vehicle and ran over to the car resting in the ditch.

"Is everyone alright?" Berry said, as he climbed up so that he could see into the driver's side window.

"I don't know, I think I broke my arm," Janice said from the passenger seat. Both girls were jumbled up together, along with the trash that composed a large percentage of the inside of the vehicle.

"I didn't see you," Patty said, as she untangled herself from Janice.

"Let's get you girls out and then worry about that," Berry said.

The girls climbed out through the driver's side window.

"My mom is going to kill me, patty moaned, starting to cry.

"Call it in, Charlie."

A few minutes later a sheriff's car pulled up, Deputy Larry Swanson stepped out.

"Howdy Mike, Charlie. Running people off the road?" Deputy Larry, Swanson called out. He surveyed the scene and could tell from the girls' expressions that they were more scared than hurt.

"Actually, more of an accident. That's a bad turn there," Charlie said.

"Anybody hurt?"

"Passenger probably has a broken arm."

The deputy walked over, spoke to the girls, and looked at Janice's arm.

"I'm sorry, I didn't see them," Patty blurted out.

"I wasn't driving," Janice quickly said.

"I just said I was driving, Janice," Patty said.

"Okay, Okay. First, let's get you both looked at and fix that arm up." Swanson led the girls to his squad, and put them both in the back seat.

"You guys can get a tow when I call TJ in a minute."

"Game's on in an hour, Swanny," Mike said.

"Yah, Yah, he'll be right out. Just enjoy nature until he gets here," Swanson said making a few quick notes. "Failure to yield, kids driving too fast. Good thing nobody was hurt. I'm sure insurance will pay for a new truck."

"Good thing it was the old truck and not the new one," Charlie said.

"That at least is something," Mike said, looking at the smashed front end of his truck. "I didn't see her, and she didn't see me, that's for damn sure," he added.

"I need to piss," Charlie said as he walked over to the side of the road.

"Good for you Charlie. I'm sure I would have figured that out," Mike said.

"I'm like a damn well-oiled machine." As he unzipped his pants, Charlie glanced down and saw a glass pipe and a scrap of foil.

"Mike, quit throwing your pot pipe on the ground. I'm always picking up after you."

"Like hell. Those girls throw it down? It looks like it hasn't been there long."

The men examined the pipe and some small scraps of residue remaining in the tinfoil.

"That, my friend, ain't pot," Mike said.

"What is it?"

"No idea. We'll drop it off at the bunker and let them figure it out."

"Fantastic, there's TJ. Let's get him to take us first. You know valuable evidence must be delivered to law enforcement."

"Technically, we're law enforcement."

"No, we keep the world safe from wildlife offenders, we're animal cops. Remember that if you're ever called to help track an armed felon."

"Unless he's dragging a poached deer I'll leave it to the pros, Mikey."

"Fantastic."

The two conservation officers leaned against the counter just inside the sheriff's station. Deputy Swanson walked over from his desk in the day room where a couple of the other deputies were writing reports. The small glass tube and crumpled tin-foil lay on the counter inside a small zip-lock evidence bag.

"I think Sam's going to want to see this," Deputy Swanson said as he picked up the pipe and foil.

"What is it, Swanny?"

"Meth, almost for sure."

"You think it was those two girls, they're sixteen, maybe seventeen."

"Happened before in Patience. Beer and pot must not be doing it anymore," Swanson said.

"Dumb ass kids."

"Didn't you do dumb ass shit when you were a kid?" Swanson asked.

"When he wasn't pissing."

"Did I ever tell you your wife worships my ass, Mikey?"

"And yours talks to a mummified lump of shit she keeps in her pocket," Charlie said as he put Mike in a friendly headlock.

"She's your sister, buddy."

Swanson rolled his eyes and shook his head. He's known these guys forever. They were inseparable and never changed. They seemed happy with their lives; anymore easy going and they'd be inert.

"I'm glad you guys spend most of your time in the park. Now take off. I'm going to drive over to Sam's and tell him about this stuff. Who knows what he'll do. He's not a big fan of drugs. The last druggy who tried to sell anything but pot here turned up two counties over, covered head to toe in bug bites ranting about wolves and black giants chasing him through the woods."

"Must have been sampling his own wares," Mike said a huge smile on his face. There was only one black giant in Patience, his buddy Nathan.

"Without a doubt," Swanson said.

"Yep, no crime in Patience."

"Fantastic," Swanson said, as he walked back towards his car.

Deputy Swanson opened his car door just as Sam came out of his house and onto the porch.

"Sam, I've got something here you'll want to see. We just found it near an accident scene. Two girls plowed into Mike and Charlie out by the state park road. I think one of them must have tossed this to the side."

"Who had this?" Sam said to his deputy when Swanson handed over the plastic bag containing the pipe and scrap of tin-foil. He was so angry that his hand was shaking as he held it. Swanson had seen Sam come unglued a couple of times. Only one rule when that happened: get out of the way!

"We think Janice Marty and Patty Pitcher."

"Those two are thick as thieves. They should know better. Why can't kids just steal their parent's beer from time to time and leave this stuff alone? I hate this shit!" Sam yelled as he walked around to the back of the squad and opened the trunk tossing the pipe into a plastic evidence box.

"I didn't mean to interrupt your day off, Sam," Swanson said as he noticed Nathan, Christine and Yves sitting on Sam's deck.

"It's okay," Sam said, trying to calm down. As Sam walked back towards the deck, Swanson could tell that he was getting agitated. He was just glad that he wasn't on the other side of that agitation.

Sam took Christine and Yves back to the restaurant, then drove on to the hospital where the 'meth girls', as Sam called them, had been taken. As he drove he remembered the disappointment on Christine's face when he told her that he had to go to work. She understood though, and asked him to stop by the restaurant later. He couldn't wait to see her again and it had only been a few minutes.

Sam jumped into his squad and called Nathan on his cell phone. "Nathan, you busy? We've got meth issues again. I'll be right over to pick you up."

Sam and Nathan pulled up to the old hospital where virtually all of Patience had been born. The building was old, but solidly built. Both the local clinic and the emergency room were part of the same building. Critical cases were airlifted to St. Louis from the helicopter pad located on top of the hospital wing. The locals said a little silent prayer to themselves each time they heard the helicopter. It meant that some friend or neighbor was in a bad way.

Sam and Nathan walked into the emergency room area and up to the front desk, where a gray haired old Doctor stood examining a file while nurses and clerical staff came and went doing the business of the busy facility.

Squad in the shop, Samson?" old Doctor Parsons said, looking up. "No accidents lately?"

Nathan jumped right in, pretending to steer a car with his hands over his eyes and smiling, to the immediate joy of the girls behind the counter.

"All in the pursuit of justice, placing myself bodily on the line to keep the world safe for democracy," Sam said, spreading his arms.

"What's up there, Samson?" the older man said.

"Just Sam, Doc, please."

"I delivered you Samson Trunce and I will call you by your Christian name if I please. And as for you Nathan, I believe I put in an order some time ago. Are you a lazy bootlegger or what?"

"Doc, I didn't hear that," Sam said.

"I am eighty years old, and was shot at more times than you've had hot dinners as a medic saving reckless young men like you during the war. I can and will prescribe whatever medication for myself that I see fit!" Doctor Parsons was at that point in his life where he didn't care if the Commander in Chief told him he couldn't have some homemade whiskey.

Sam raised his hands in mock supplication. "I need a blood draw from those two girls that were just brought in."

"I already drew the driver for a tox scan. Accident case you know there Sheriff. What am I going to find?"

"Methamphetamine, I think."

"In a child I delivered? That will not stand!" Dr. Parsons said raising his voice and tossing the file he was reading down in contempt.

"I plan to nail this one right away. Wherever the supply is coming from, I'm going to burn the bastards down."

Doctor Parsons just nodded and laid his hand on Sam's shoulder. "Any help I can give, Sam."

"How long for a lab result?"

"Week or so," Doctor Parsons said.

"Too long. It's time for the direct approach," Sam said.

"Are you going to call their parents first?" Doc Parsons asked.

"No, I know both of their parents and they're better off telling me first. We'll all tell their parents together. I am not going to wait. Besides, I'm not going to prosecute these girls if they cooperate. They got hurt, Mike and Charlie are alright."

"You know what's best, Sam. Call me if you need me."

"Let's go there, Gentle Ben," Sam said moving back towards the hospital examination rooms.

"I feel all jittery and my arm hurts like hell. When do you think they'll tell us we can go?" Janice whined. "It feels like the walls are closing in on us," Janice said, adjusting her cast in the sling holding her arm immobile.

"I know what you mean. I want to get out of here, like now. You should ask them for some pain meds and save one for me. That stuff really kicks ass."

Just as she spoke the door opened and Sam and Nathan walked in. The room was small enough so that Nathan pretty much took up the available space. He leaned on the examination table and stared at the girls as he picked his teeth with a tooth pick. His teeth looked like an entire accordion keyboard.

"Girls," Sam sighed. "I thought you were smarter than that."

"What, sheriff? It was just an accident," Patty said.

"Meth pipes, your blood positive for meth, an injured passenger. One, two, three, prison," Sam continued sitting down onto the examination table.

"One two three," Nathan nodded in affirmation. "The old one, two, three: a prison guarantee!"

"I wasn't driving," Janice blurted out.

"Shut up, Janice."

"Show 'em how to make a shiv out of a spoon, Sam," Nathan said and made stabbing motions in the air over the girls' heads. "Can't send 'em in with the big bitch without a shiv."

"The big bitch?" Patty questioned.

"Almost as big as Nathan. She loves the tender teenage meat. She runs the women's prison over at Charity," Sam said as if he was reading a brochure.

"She the warden?" Patty asked her voice shaking.

"Warden! The warden doesn't actually go to the prison, too dangerous. She more like calls it in and makes sure the food and supplies are pushed through the gate. The big bitch is the main bull, you know, guard. Anyway, you'll learn all the lingo." Sam locked eyes with Patty.

"You're just trying to scare us. Kids don't go to prison."

"What are you, seventeen now? You're almost an adult anyway. I'm sure they'd try you as an adult. Yah, I'd dress like a kid if I were you when I went in front of the judge, he hates druggies."

"Sam, you forgot the finger prints," Nathan said, wagging a sausage-like finger at Sam.

Both girls were pale and too terrified to cry. Sam knew he'd pushed enough, so he let a little light into their world of misery.

"Now, I might be able to keep the judge from going, you know, side two when he hears, but I'm going to need a little help."

"What do we have to do?" Janice said.

"I need to know where you got the meth."

"You mean narc?" Patty answered.

"Everyone is the big bitch's narc, everyone," Nathan said rolling his eyes around.

"Henry!" both girls said in unison.

"Henry the head, old hemp boy?" Sam growled.

"Don't tell him we said so," Patty added.

Sam looked at the girls and said, "Let me point something out to you. You are seventeen years old and think all adults don't know anything. All adults were once your age. Do you think people just magically get stupid once they're over thirty? Are you going to jump off a damn cliff when you're thirty Patty?"

"No," Patty said sliding down in her chair.

Why not? You'll just be a stupid, useless old bag."

"I don't think adults are stupid," Patty murmured.

"Of course you do. Didn't any adult ever tell you meth was bad?"

"In school."

"Do you think they told you not to use it so that there would be more for themselves?"

Both girls shook their heads.

"You see, believe it or not, you do learn some things as you get older. Adult life is hard work, so don't spend the last few years of real freedom you have putting Drano into your bodies," Sam said.

"Drano?"

"Drano, Lye, Muriatic acid, matchstick heads, and industrial solvents all that crap are used to make meth. What, you think meth is produced in a high tech lab somewhere? Most meth labs are in places you wouldn't drive by if you had the choice. Most of the people that sell the shit don't use it. You know why? Because they're crooked adults and they're smarter than you. They'll take your dumb ass money though."

"Are we going to jail now?" Janice said in a small voice.

"We are going to your house and we are going to talk to your parents. I will be there to make sure you get your story straight. You mess up at all and I hear about it, you will end up in Charity. Never was a place so improperly named."

"Are you going to tell anyone else?" Patty said.

"No, and neither are you. This is between you and me." Sam stood up and abruptly left the room. Nathan waited a minute and moved towards the door.

"You have no idea how close you came. By the way, you piss off Sam, you better just go and stay gone. I watched him deck the big bitch once with one punch and then spit on her," Nathan added.

"What for?" Janice asked, her eyes darting back and forth.

"Stepped on his foot. He doesn't like her much," Nathan said as he slid through the open door sideways and left.

"Henry the head. You've been too lenient Sam," Nathan said from the back seat of the squad as they drove out of the hospital parking lot.

"That's nice coming from you, Jack Daniels. I swear to god you're like the Good Humor ice cream man tinkling down the street with your customers following along: "where's my jug, where's my jug?""

"I distill only the best for my customers."

"The best lethal, caustic rocket fuel known to man, you mean. After a nuclear war, there'll be nothing but cockroaches and jugs of that chrome cleaner laying around. Thanks for your help. Despite your obvious faults, I appreciate your helping me grab these idiots from time to time."

"Glad to help the man who's taking me to dinner. By the way, swing by my house. I need to pick something up for the proprietress." Both men just sniggered and laughed. They had grown up, but remembered when they were full of piss and vinegar and the whole of their lives seemed to lay ahead, catching fish, chasing girls and lions. They'd known it all once, too.

CHAPTER
TWELVE

Carlos stood quietly, waiting for Jose to acknowledge his presence and permit him to speak. This was a new rule and destined to result in pushing Carlos even closer to the edge. He fantasized about Jose's death frequently now, and the wonderful, almost innumerable ways he could carry it out.

"Patron, Doc has prepared a quantity of the product," Carlos said.

"It is time to move some of it," Jose answered. "We'll start small and then build the operation into several labs."

Jose was in the middle of piecing together a beautiful Italian Berretta shotgun that he had just taken apart to clean, and was doing just about everything backwards, trying not to appear too frustrated.

"I would be pleased to do that for you, Patron," Carlos offered.

"My uncle always says that a man should handle his own firearms so that he knows them like fine wine or a beautiful woman," Jose said airily as he idly reached down and stroked his dog's ears. Lion was in the middle of a snap fest trying to catch a fly as it buzzed around his head. A damn avalanche could fall on that mutt's head and he'd never know it, Carlos thought.

"When we are fully operational, then we will distribute our product. Most of it will go to St. Louis, the rest locally. We must build our market and establish our territory."

"It might be best not to attract attention in the rural areas where we manufacture, Patron."

"I have already begun a modest local distribution. We must build our centers of influence."

"I really think..." Carlos interrupted.

"That is why you are not in charge. You lack the business skill and high intellect for such matters," Jose snapped dismissively.

I can snap a simple shotgun together, as well as keep a low profile Carlos thought. I really need reassignment he told himself, not for the first time that day.

"We will create an epidemic and feed the sickness. I will build an empire and go back to Mexico to take over when my uncle is ready." Jose had risen and that's when Carlos noticed the piece of toilet paper stuck to his shoe, trailing behind him, so had the dog. Carlos could see the tension building in the animal. It obviously thought some vicious white creature had attached itself to his master. It would soon be gun time, Carlos decided.

"I will attend to it immediately," Carlos said, as he almost ran from the room. Just as he closed the door he heard a wild howl, and in his mind's eye could picture the dog leaping across the room at the creature attacking his master's shoe. He cringed as he awaited the gunshot, but none came. When he peeked into the room Jose was holding the gun and looking down into the barrel. He quickly closed the door again and made a silent prayer, which had nothing to do with God preventing an accident.

CHAPTER
THIRTEEN

"Time to find Henry the Head," Sam said to three of his deputies sitting around in what Sam liked to call the ready room back at the Sheriff's station. There was a large map of Patience County on one wall, a conference table and a couple of old couches where most of the discussions took place. A sliding glass window separated the room from the day room.

"He's washing dishes at the Fish 'n Feet over in Jackson," Lisa called from her desk.

"The Fish n Feet?" Taylor Marshall said. He was Sam's new deputy, fresh out of the military and law Enforcement College.

"It's really Bob's Surf 'n Turf, but about twenty-five years ago, some mobsters dumped some other mobster's feet off in the dumpster behind the restaurant. The name kind of stuck. Fish isn't bad, couldn't tell you about the feet," Sam said.

"That's technically out of our jurisdiction, Sheriff," Taylor said.

"You know, I hate that word. If some clowns are moving meth in Patience, I don't care where they land. You know hot pursuit," Sam smiled.

"How's that, Sheriff?" Taylor cautiously said. He knew plenty about command structure and when to tread lightly.

"When Henry sees me coming there'll be hot pursuit alright. I warned the puke. So what does he do? He sets up shop just inside the next county, sells pot so the cops really don't give a shit. You try to be nice and it never fails. Maybe my message wasn't sincere enough before. I'll have to be more direct."

Henry the Head Walker stood in the dumpster enclosure out back behind the restaurant, smoking a roach and a cigarette simultaneously. He wasn't doing much to hide it. He could have been an escaped convict for all his employer cared, as long as the dishes got done and he kept up.

"Oh Henry," Sam called from the other side of the dumpster like a mother calling her kid in for dinner.

"Shit," Henry hissed and tossed the smoldering roach into his mouth and almost immediately starting to cough and choke.

"Let me know when the fire's out. Take your time," Sam said sticking his head in between the swinging doors that allowed access for dumping grease and garbage.

"Why are you harassing me? I'm not doing anything wrong!" Henry wailed.

"That's not what a couple of teens over in Patience tell me. Graduated to meth, prison time for Henry," Sam said sliding through the doors.

"I don't know what you're talking about, Sheriff."

Sam lifted the lid on a fifty five gallon drum of kitchen grease. "Yummy. Ever slip and accidentally dunk your head into the grease here."

"Don't you touch me, Sheriff. There's a camera pointing over at the dumpster here," Henry blurted out nervously.

"Right now that camera is getting a lovely shot of Nathan's back. Have you ever stood behind him in a line? It's like your whole world becomes Nathan's stinking back. You can't see around him, under him, over him. He's a damn billboard, and that's what the camera sees."

"Fuck you."

The very next second Henry knew he had made a mistake. Sam took his head and plunged it into the drum. Henry struggled furiously, but he felt like a mouse under a cat's paw. He was near panic. Panic arrived in the form of the song Sam started to sing.

"Hold the pickle; hold the lettuce, special orders don't upset us…"

Sam yanked Henry's head out of the grease. "You better not get any on my clothes boy!"

"Okay! Okay!"

Sam lifted the lid on the dumpster and pulled out some wadded up towels and napkins so the kid could at least wipe the grime from his eyes.

"You could have killed me!"

"I saved you. You passed out from that dope in your system and were unlucky enough to fall into the grease barrel. They'll make me a hero, marching bands, girls throwing themselves at my feet!"

The kid stood there with his mouth open, watching Sam gesticulate, spreading his arms like he was receiving an Academy Award. That was all he needed to see.

"I got it from a Mexican guy who came into the restaurant, just a little to try. I gave it to those girls. I was hoping for a little action," Henry said mournfully.

"I didn't hear that, Henry. Once you're out of high school the buffet is closed. You guys are all the same. You drive the same beater Camaro, go to the same high school parties and try to hustle sophomores. You're supposed to leave and go see the world."

"You did, and you came back."

"I just didn't like what I saw. Besides, I have to keep the world safe from meth boys like you."

"Now what, Sheriff?" Henry said miserably.

"I need to meet Pancho Villa."

"Who?"

"Your Mexican friend," Sam said.

"His name isn't Pancho."

Sam shook his head. "Pancho Villa was a Mexican bandit and freedom fighter. Just trying to lighten the mood for you a bit, no? No comprendo?"

"He told me he'd have more for me next Friday after my shift, said more was coming in."

"Time?" Sam demanded.

"After nine," Henry said.

"I'll be here. Nathan too, we'll sit out on the new patio. It's better for Nathan to sit outside, puts some people off."

"Mostly jealous husbands and boyfriends when their women respond to my royal bearing," Nathan rumbled.

"Either that or the bone yard you create around your table," Sam suggested.

Henry looked past Sam at Nathan. That's when he noticed the enormous spear Nathan had in his hand.

"Now Henry, you tell anyone about our discussion and you'll be lucky to survive arrest. I'll put you in prison and tell your cell mate that you're an informer and a child molester."

"I'm no child molester."

"I know, but so what?" Sam said.

Henry was done. "Whatever you say Sheriff," he said, defeated.

"Good man. Now get yourself cleaned up, and pull that French fry from behind your ear. You're part of a team here, at the Feet. Show some damn pride." Somewhere along the line Sam had shifted into his George C. Scott, Patton impression. Nathan had started to dance, humming the Burger King jingle. Henry fled back into the restaurant.

"Fine young man, fine young man," Sam said sagely as they wandered over to the squad.

CHAPTER
FoURTEEN

B ehind a pile of bones, Nathan chewed methodically. Sam and John had finished their meals, and sat sipping coffee and watching. The sight never got old. While the two of them were splattered and smeared, and had worn old shirts to dinner, Nathan remained spotless. The sauce never had a chance.

It's getting close to nine. Remember, we're here to work," John said looking at his watch.

"That's why we're not drinking beer, Dad," Sam said.

"That water you Americans call beer," Nathan laughed.

"I like my beer to only have been in my mouth and nobody else's," Sam answered, referring to the Masai traditional brew, where the grain was pre-chewed by the tribe's women to start the fermentation process.

Nathan pushed aside his plate at last. "Alright, let's go over the plan."

"Dad, you just leave and hang back and watch out backs. Please, nothing heavy, even if things get bad."

"This is just a snatch job, right? As I see it, the guy we grab will probably only have a little meth, but some info we need," John said pretending not to hear Sam's request.

"Yes sir, but things seem to get hairy fast when meth is involved. I saw a few bad things in Detroit. These guys on it get dementia, they believe everyone is a cop and out to get them." Sam didn't have to mention that it had been a drug related bust that had nearly killed him.

"We'll all be on our toes, Sam," Nathan said. He had gone into his warrior mode and Sam saw it right away. There would be no more goofing around. It happened every time Sam referred to his Detroit days. It had been Nathan's influence as much as anyone's that had brought him home. He'd gone to the hospital in Detroit the night Sam was shot. The night Sam was supposed to die. The night John Trunce threatened to kill the priest who had come to give Sam's last rites if he didn't leave. When Sam pulled through, Nathan explained the misery that John had gone through and told him that if he was a man he would realize that finding oneself had nothing to do with where you were geographically, and that if he insisted on dying to save people, they should at least be people he loved and who loved him. John had been so grief-stricken that many of his friends, few of whom knew Sam, had come to visit him at the hospital.

Nathan asked Sam if he didn't want that kind of devotion from at least one man other than he. Nathan never had any problems expressing to Sam how he felt. They were warrior brothers, and those weren't just words, not to the Masai.

"You are my brother, Nathan," Sam said, as he clasped Nathan on the shoulder.

"You are Masai Sam."

"Remember your training, men," John said.

"Let's go to work," Sam said.

Without any further discussion, Nathan found a dark spot and Sam blended into the shadows by the dumpster. Henry had already been instructed to come out and walk over to the vehicle that his supplier was driving. Before the meal, Sam had met with Henry, who told him that his supplier would be driving a nondescript blue sedan, the type of car that wouldn't attract attention.

After a few minutes, Henry came out the back door of the restaurant and slung a bag of trash into the dumpster. Sam saw a blue, four door Ford pull into the parking lot. Henry walked over to the driver's side door. Sam watched closely as Henry exchanged a few words with the driver, who tossed a crumpled fast food bag in the direction of the dumpster. Henry walked over to the bag, picked it up and wedged it under the dumpster lid. The driver put the vehicle into gear and suddenly his rear end was lifted into the air.

"Howdy amigos! Commo estas?" Sam said, leaning against the car and pointing a .9 mm pistol inside.

"Nice night for a drug delivery," Nathan bellowed.

"We don't have any drugs, Jeffe," the driver claimed.

"No drugs, Nathan," Sam said.

"Keys, please, and put it in park," Sam said. It was then that the two men noticed that Sam's gun had a silencer screwed into the end. That caught their attention. Few cops carried silenced weapons. In their experience, they were only carried by killers.

"Drugs?" Sam said.

"No Drugs," the passenger said.

"Nathan."

With what seemed to take no more effort than shrugging, Nathan simply rolled the car over, causing surprising little sound.

"Shit, shit," the driver said. "The only drugs were in that bag, man," he said pointing to the bag Henry had pushed into the garbage can.

"Well you better climb on out. If one of you makes any kind of move, I'll shoot you," Sam said, lifting his badge out from under his shirt.

"Don't make us go out there man, it'll be bad," the passenger said. The men seemed spooked and nervous.

By this time Nathan had walked around to the passenger side, reached in, and yanked the passenger out by his right arm. Sam stuck the silencer in the driver's ear as he was crawling out.

"I'm coming, don't shoot."

Sam swiftly patted the guy down and had him lie on the ground. He looked over to see Nathan holding the passenger by one ankle and shaking him upside down, while he frisked him with his other hand. Change, a spare clip, a comb, lint, everything was spilling out of the terrified guy's pockets. Nathan found a small automatic. He dropped the guy mostly on his shoulders and put his enormous bare foot in the small of his back. Both men were glancing around wildly.

"These guys are spooked. Let's get over to the squad." As Sam spoke he heard a door slide open and the action of an automatic weapon being engaged.

"Cover!" Sam yelled as he dove in the direction of a garbage can. Nathan dove in the other direction, rolling over the bottom of the car. Their immediate action saved them both, as at least two full on automatic weapons sprayed the area where they had been standing. The two drug dealers didn't react as quickly and were both hit numerous times as they tried to scramble off the pavement.

Both Sam and Nathan returned fire, as a white van with its side door open sped past, slammed on its brakes, and turned for another pass.

Sam and Nathan were still exposed, and without any further thought, Nathan ran over and picked Sam up, threw him over his shoulder, and ran.

John had seen the exchange from his vantage point. He watched in awe as Nathan scooped up his son and ran from the parking lot towards a hill covered with oaks and maples. It was like watching a big cat chasing down its prey. Nathan moved with alarming speed, hit the hill, and actually accelerated up the slope. The only other person John had ever seen accelerate from a dead run was Carl Lewis, in the hundred meters. Nathan could have taken Carl that night, carrying Sam, while being shot at. The soldier John Trunce acted while the man John Trunce took in the scene. Without hesitation, he flipped up the back seat of his jeep, took out a cylindrical object and sighted in on the van. Just as the van spun around in front of a corn field a short distance down the road from the access road to the restaurant, he fired. A rocket streamed out of the weapon and slammed into the side of the van and detonated. The van exploded into tiny pieces and rained down onto the corn field. John calmly packed the weapon back into its compartment, just as Nathan ran up, dropped Sam into the front seat and jumped in the back himself. John immediately turned the jeep uphill, away from the road, and took off.

"Damn it Nathan, I can run you know!" Sam said, more as a statement than in anger.

"Of course you can," was all Nathan said by way of explanation.

"What the hell was that Dad?" Sam said, obviously referring to the rocket blast.

"Panzerfauste," John said as the jeep bounced all over what was once a trail. His eyes were ablaze and mischievous.

"That wouldn't be a World War Two German anti-tank weapon, would it?" Sam asked.

"Yep, the 60. Effective against all Allied tanks in the war, even the giant Russian bastards, the Stalins."

"Good to know they're effective against heavily armored minivans," Sam replied.

"You were compromised, soldier. Didn't you hear? Those were Kalishnokovs, AK 47 assault rifles. It would have been a one-sided firefight with innocent people around, so I took them out."

"You were not here, Dad. The official story is gonna be the old hot round in the gas tank excuse, because I know I'll get a call from the sheriff over in Jackson County. I know him, and he's a good man, but he'll have something to say."

The next day Sam was sitting in the bunker when the phone rang.

"Goddamn anti-tank Sam," Sheriff Baker said in an almost pleading voice.

"No, it must have been a hot round in the tank," Sam offered.

"Sure Sam. Just so you know, about an hour ago nine guys, that's nine, Sam, in black suits and black Ray Ban sunglasses showed up for a chat. I know a damn spook when I see one. Hopefully these guys were from our government. They were everywhere; I mean we were scared shitless. These bastards were cold killers. If that wasn't enough, after they were here for about twenty minutes, hands down the scariest dude I have ever seen walked into the station. He must have been their fearless leader. He was like six foot four, black hair, black eyes, no smile. I swear the temperature in the room dropped ten degrees. I'm still not completely convinced that the guy wasn't death himself, masquerading as a government agent to amuse himself and kill time until he grabbed his next million souls. He politely thanked me for turning over all data on the incident and informed me that as a matter of national security nobody would speak about it again. He said if there was a breach of security I could expect him back. I turned around for a second, and he was gone, just gone. Like smoke in a hurricane. Buddy of yours?"

"I have no clue," Sam lied. Jackson's sheriff had just met his brother, Tracy.

Tracy Trunce set down the phone in his office at NSA headquarters in Washington and shredded a small file that contained all references to the incident in Jackson County. Tracy was a senior NSA officer and intervened in modest ways in his family's doings in Patience, mostly gathering information and coordinating with Bill "Moon" Meyer, one of his former NSA agents, now relocated to Patience in a quasi-witness protection situation. Moon would have been a valuable capture by any foreign government, friendly or not, not so much for what he knew, but for what he could do. There simply weren't any other cryptographers of his caliber. He was a genius at most disciplines that he applied himself to: math, computer science, chemistry and physics. The list of sciences that he'd conquered was lengthy, but his true passion was weaponry. He and John Trunce had become fast friends after his move to Patience, often sneaking off like two kids to play with fireworks, except that their fireworks were things like Panzerfaustes.

"Sam," Tracy said into the phone connected to a scrambled line.

"Trace!" Sam said with great enthusiasm.

"A Panzerfauste?"

"I swear I had no idea. All we were trying to do was roust a couple of Mexican meth boys and show them the error of their ways. Their display of firepower means they were heavy hitters."

"We'll check the usual sources to see if there's been any discernible communication pattern increase to any of the known Mexican mob heads. Sometimes they have little idea of what their people are doing on the ground. Meth is a big export from Mexico, and like most really bad drugs out there, the guys who are making it in quantity and moving it don't use it," Tracy said.

"That should be the biggest clue to the people attracted to it: the people who have an endless supply would only use it at gunpoint. It must be a great source of amusement to them to sell so much of it to the Anglos," Sam pointed out.

"Tell dad to try to avoid further use of ordinance, although I suppose it's a good thing that he wasn't up in his thunderbolt at the time."

"I'll try to discourage any possibility of it," Sam said.

"I think you guys should formulate a defensive plan. Whoever tried to put holes in you isn't going to like the loss of personnel, weaponry, product, or money."

"We're getting the word out. I think they'll have to do a little recon. I'm sure they'll get to Henry the Head; he's gondi."

"I might bug out too, after I see a Panzerfauste take out a minivan, must have been a sight, Tracy said."

"The pieces are still falling."

After his call with Tracy, Sam called the station and spoke to Lisa.

"Spread the word, meeting at Madeleine's. I want all the deputies to be told and to round up the usual suspects." That was Sam's fun way of saying to round up their friends who represented decades of combat experience.

Sam hung up the phone and dialed Madeleine's number. More than once, important meetings were held in the basement of her restaurant. When Sam and his friends were ridding Patience of the meth dealers who had sprung up prior to his return, strategy meetings were held there. Sam knew that this time they were dealing with an unknown entity. Before, it had been disorganized thugs who were dealt with. Someone had upped the ante this time.

"Madeleine, Sam here. We have a situation; we need to hold a meeting today."

"Eight o'clock in the basement. We will not be disturbed."

Sam was always surprised that she acted in such a business-like fashion when it came to these potentially dangerous situations. Sam's family and friends took their way of life and safety very seriously; this extended to their community. It was an unspoken, collective effort to create some kind of haven of right in a world of increasing wrong. They fought back.

Madeleine hung up the phone and sighed. She had been struggling her whole life against oppression. She stood and looked out the window overlooking the brook, thinking back to the years of her youth when she glowed with the physical beauty that her granddaughter shared. Aside from that, their lives had been very different. She had been a young, carefree girl living a modest but comfortable life with her parents when the German army suddenly took France and the life of her brother, for whom she still cried. When she was sad she still remembered swimming with him and playing on the beach in La Ciotat on their summer holidays. When he died, summer was over and she found her way into the Resistance. She was trained by the British Special Operations Executive, boys whose country was being turned to rubble by the Germans. She learned to kill without hesitation or remorse. Learning to fight and to use a knife and other weapons came quickly. She never had to learn not to hesitate. Every face of every German was an insult to her brother and to France. She participated in countless raids, blew up supply trains, and killed German officers. She was the most proud of her work hiding Jewish children from the Nazis. After the war many of these children tracked her down, all the way to Patience. During the war she had been hunted by the enemy relentlessly and was constantly on the move. She had earned the nickname 'The Angel of Death.'

She was hard on collaborators, some of whom she killed for treason, women and men she knew or had grown up with. Once the Allies came and France was liberated, she resurfaced and tried to return to her life, but the collaborators and many of the people in her community were either afraid of her or didn't know how to relate to the person the war had turned her into.

She could not remain in France and left with her new husband initially for England and then the United States. Her husband, Jack Teach had been a British Special Operations Officer, and the head of the training division. Both he and then others prepared her for the three years she operated as an assassin. Jack never treated her as anything other than a soldier. The training had been painful and hard, and they formed a bond. On her first assignment they were together and encountered a patrol that would have discovered the bombs they had just carefully lain on the train tracks to take out a train moving munitions. Teach pointed to the two German soldiers and to himself and her. He gave her a look she remembered even after his death: pure confidence. The two moved from the shadows as the Germans passed, each killing their target silently and dragging them off the track. Teach hadn't congratulated her, patted her on the back or in any way demonstrated to her that she had passed some test or baptism of fire. It was the greatest compliment he could have given her, his respect. It was she that came to him the night before he was to leave to train others. Their love was passionate and abrupt. Afterwards, they spoke and talked of everything but the war. He told her he would see her again if he wasn't killed, and she believed him.

It was the week the Allies crossed into Germany, and she was no longer at risk. She was working with her mother in the kitchen when she saw him through the window, tall, handsome, and all shoulders, walking towards her gate wearing his full uniform. She quietly set down the knife that she was peeling potatoes with, ran through the front door and into his arms. Before he said hello, he asked her to marry him. She kissed him yes. She led him by the hand back into the house and collected her parents. They walked to the church, found the priest, and were married, remaining that way until his death a couple of years ago.

She'd taken his ashes back to France. Alone she walked off into the countryside to place them along the side of an old railroad track, long since unused, a memory, like the war, all but forgotten except by the people who had lived it and put their family and friends in the ground because of it.

Over the years she'd visited her hometown more and more. The pain had dulled and the faces changed. It was funny how she and her husband had decided to move to America to a place called Patience, all on the say so of one crazy American paratrooper, no more than a boy.

The group in the basement of the restaurant sat around one of the heavy oak tables that was used upstairs and brought out when larger gatherings required it. Sam loved the basement. It was full of bottles of wine, sausages and peppers hanging from the ceiling. On the shelves were big cans of imported olive oil, onions, garlic, and truffles all blending into a fragrance that whispered a promise of exceptional cuisine.

Madeleine, John Trunce and his wife, Nathan, his father and mother, TJ, Sam, Moon, and a heavyset man named Martin, 'Davy' Crockett, a local used car salesman and Vietnam veteran, were all gathered. Just as everybody sat down, Christine and Yves came down carrying a ceramic jug of wine and glasses.

Yves sat next to his grandmother. Christine set the jug down in the middle of the table, along with some bread and cheese, and took a seat on the bench right next to Sam. A few people smiled a little, mostly at the flash of surprise that crossed Sam's face.

"Samson, let's hear what you've got," John Trunce began.

Sam gave a detailed explanation of what they knew so far. It wasn't much.

"How do you think we should handle it?" TJ asked.

"We all need to be on the lookout for strangers and to spread the word around. It shouldn't be too hard to spot Mexican gang members. We don't exactly have a huge Hispanic population," Nathan said.

"It's a mistake to assume that this gang is all Hispanic or that they aren't sophisticated enough to not attract attention," John said.

"If they spend any amount of time here, they will end up either getting gas or buying food. We'll watch for them where they are most likely to go. If cars come into town and just drive around without stopping anywhere, that's out of the ordinary and will need watching," Sam added.

"When will the dogs come?" Nathan's mother asked. She was dressed in a brilliant red Kanga signifying the power of her tribe. Her posture and bearing were unmistakably royal, completely at ease in a council of war, ready to embrace bloodshed without fear.

"It depends how pissed off they are that their van got Panzerfausted," Sam said.

"A Panzerfauste? My compliments, John," Madeleine said with a slight smile.

"If something works, stick with it," John agreed.

There was some more discussion and the wine and cheese were attacked. Soon, Sam called an end to the meeting and followed the group upstairs. Only John and Madeleine stayed behind.

"Up in a second," John said as his wife glanced back.

"We should try to do this with a minimum of casualties, Madeleine"

"John, I think you may have already moved this thing beyond that," she said without reproach.

"They fired automatic weapons on Sam and Nathan. I will kill all of them if they come for any of the people I love."

"As will I," Madeleine said as she raised a glass to the other pure warrior in the room.

CHAPTER
FIFTEEN

Doc and Billy sat in a thicket of brush swatting flies and kept an eye on Henry the Head's trailer. It was a miserable excuse for any kind of structure, much less a dwelling. They had been sitting there awhile and the flies seemed to be getting thicker. Doc moved the metal lawn chair he had appropriated from a near-by home as far from Billy as possible. Virgil lay prone, watching the trailer through cheap binoculars. Doc had cut Billy off from any meth until after their little meeting with Henry. He was beginning to question the wisdom of his decision. He was sure Billy was picking and eating the scabs on his arm, searching for a little taste of meth to tide him over. He couldn't believe it, but he had seen a meth addict do that once during a short stay in a county jail in Iowa. The guy had not only eaten every one of his own scabs, but had offered to purchase another inmate's for consumption. After seeing that, he never had to remind himself how really bad meth was.

To avoid puking himself, Doc was considering giving, Billy the Scab Cannibal, a mini-dose to guarantee his attention. The need immediately disappeared when Billy saw Henry ride up on a bicycle that seemed to be at least two sizes too small for him. Billy charged before Doc could even stand up. Despite his considerable mass, Billy moved like an orca attacking a seal. He flew into Henry, smashing him to the ground.

"Don't kill him, Billy," Doc said.

Billy looked up at him with vacant eyes as he sat on Henry the Head's head.

"That's all I know. All I said was that those two dudes were coming later. I don't know anything about you guys and I don't want to know," was the muffled plea from Henry.

"The Sheriff, Sam Trunce, and a giant black dude? The sheriff maybe, but a giant black guy?" Doc said skeptically.

"Wait until you see the dude. You'll need an army if you go after that monster. I've heard lots of stories about Trunce. He's flat out crazy. The last guy who tried to sell anything other than pot over there ended up in the nut house, babbling about being chased by wolves and African warriors. When they found him, it was only because they finally allowed him to escape after two full days of being hunted through the woods. The guy looked like he'd been through hell. Not good."

"Sounds like the sheriff thinks he's a vigilante, or Buford T Justice. We're still not sure how the van blew up, but I can tell you the higher ups are wild about it," Doc answered.

"What about me?" moaned Henry.

"You disappear," Doc said.

"Shit!"

"Not like that, you get your ass on the Dog and get gone."

"The dog?"

"The Greyhound Bus."

"Can I get up? He's shitting on my head."

"Billy has the worst ass gas going. Must be all the fast food and sugary junk he eats, when he eats. Now get going. And Henry."

"Yes?"

"You remember, like me and the other Hippies said in the old days, meth is death."

Henry was gone like a shot.

"Patron, we think the vehicle was blown up by a rocket," Carlos said simply. He'd been in a few serious gang clashes. They escalated all the time.

Jose was pacing around the room, gun in hand, gesticulating wildly. Spit was flying out of his mouth, and his eyes were like bright red saucers.

"They will all drown in pools of blood! This is war! They have blown up my loyal warriors."

Carlos knew it was more about the $100,000.00 in cash and meth that had been blown to smithereens, but he played along.

"They must be well armed. We are finding out who it was right now. It could be another gang, or dirty cops. I highly doubt they're regular law enforcement. They just don't go around blowing cars up."

"Cops can be bought."

"Not like at home, Patron."

"Well, somebody got away with blowing up a minivan with three men, money, and drugs inside, and it's not in any paper. I want those men dead. I will send my best men to quietly kill him. I think a drug overdose would be appropriate, and sufficiently embarrassing."

Carlos nodded. Miraculously, Jose was enjoying a moment of lucidity and actually making good sense.

"We should wait until Doc reports, and then you can decide what is best, Patron."

Carlos was already formulating his distancing plan regarding this situation. He thought it was best to cut their losses and move on. There was plenty of rural America to exploit. Criminals just don't get RPGed in what was supposed to be Mayberry USA, and Ol' Andy Griffin didn't run around with giant deputies who flipped over perfectly good cars. He was going to keep his opinions to himself, but he was going to let Manny the Farmer know what was going on. That was his real job. Just as he'd made up his mind on that score, his cell phone rang.

"It's me." Doc's voice came over the line.

"What do you know?"

"We've got info pointing to the Sheriff from Patience County and if it's to be believed, a giant black dude was with him and apparently picked up our mule's car and flipped it onto its roof. That of course was before the van blew," Doc said into his cell phone. He hated giving bad news to potentially hostile employers.

"I've heard some of the details. You think a rocket launcher was used?" Carlos questioned.

"I gotta say, I've messed around with a little ordinance myself. That van had some serious help blowing up. There ain't shit left."

"We need to do our own investigation. I think you need to cut your baggage loose."

"He knows nothing. I'll give him a "forget-me" cocktail and let him go."

"Any chance of using him later?"

"Anything is possible."

"Fine, then."

Carlos always kept his cell calls to seconds. He knew technology was the second best weapon law enforcement had against drug dealers. The first was getting people to not purchase the product. As far as he could tell, there had been little effort to educate people. Hell, meth had been around a long time, and had been a serious problem for years. It was only just now getting any kind of serious coverage. Funny how the media portrayed it as if it was a sudden and new threat that had just recently been discovered. Typical, the cops, the prosecutors, and the public defenders had known for years, but for most people that was a different world, the real one.

CHAPTER
SIXTEEN

It's better to keep a low profile, Sam thought as he drove one of the county sedans down to the regional Highway Patrol Station to touch base with an old friend. He felt anxious about the lack of any immediate reaction to the incident at the Fish n' Feet. He wanted to discreetly get the word out and the best way to do that was in person.

Time for a pit stop, Sam thought as he pulled off the road at a convenience store to gas up and hit the restroom. He put the gas nozzle into the tank and, while it was pumping, walked over to the restroom on the side of the building and entered. He was washing his hands when he noticed another man walk in and enter a stall. Sam was wiping his hands just as another man came in and immediately tried to hit him with a hand held Taser unit. The man's movement was too abrupt. Seeing it, Sam rushed at him and slammed him into the wall. Just as he did, the first man exploded out of the stall and stabbed at him with a hypodermic needle.

"No you don't," Sam yelled as he moved slightly to his left to avoid the needle. With his free hand he grabbed the man's wrist, plucked the needle from his grasp, and drove it into the man's leg.

"You like that?" Sam taunted.

The man screamed and tried to go for his gun. Sam managed to punch him. Out of the corner of his eye, he noticed the man with the tazer open his eyes and reach into his waistband for a gun.

Two guns against one, time to go, Sam thought as he shoved into the killer coming out of the stall, momentarily affecting his aim. The gun went off and Sam bolted out the door. Sprinting for his car, he saw his assailants' backup waiting in a van. A door slid open and a gunman with a machine pistol jumped out of the van training his weapon on Sam.

"What the hell," Sam yelled as he shot in the direction of the shooter, making him duck back inside the van and out of the line of fire. I am out gunned, Sam thought as he saw people were now reacting to the gunfire inside the store.

"Shit!" He swore shooting out the driver's side window of his car and diving through the opening. As soon as he was inside an Uzi fired again. Sam turned the key and slammed the car into drive and immediately floored the accelerator with his hand. The car shot forward and Sam squirreled himself upright in the seat, just as the gas nozzle ripped out of the pump and was dragged down the street. Uzi jumped back into the van and took off after him. Almost immediately the men in the van began to shoot wildly at the fleeing vehicle. Both vehicles shot out onto the highway careening down the road.

I've got to get away from these civilians, Sam thought deciding not to return fire until it was safe to do so. He reached for the radio and saw that the microphone had been cut from the unit. His cell was in his front pocket, and he couldn't yet get to it and drive at the same time. If he only had the squad, he thought. The one time I didn't think I needed it, I need it, he thought. He could see himself doing a bootleggers turn and ramming the bastard head on. The sedan had a six cylinder engine, but the van had clearly been modified. He just couldn't get ahead of it. Another burst took out the back window and two bullets hit the dash on the passenger side.

Sam swerved and miraculously was able to get his shoulder harness on and buckled.

"Let's see if you bastards like it off road," Sam muttered jamming the wheel to the right off the highway and plummeting down a short ditch and into a corn field. The van followed immediately and stopped about fifty feet from where Sam had barreled in. Sam leapt from the car and scrambled toward some brush and woods. Uzi seemed to have an endless supply of bullets, but Sam managed to keep the car between him and the woods. Chewing dirt the whole way, he made it into the trees and started to zigzag and take cover. Whoever was following sprayed down a barrage as they stumbled into just about every tree and rock. Sam gained some distance and took cover behind a large rock. My turn, he thought peering around the side of the rock. He saw a muzzle flash and squeezed a shot dead center. He heard a scream and more cursing.

"Come on!" Sam yelled willing them forward despite his dwindling ammunition.

Sam heard sirens wailing off in the distance. He saw the men from the van run back to it. The Van careened across the highway, straightened out and then proceeded to follow the speed limit in the direction of the sirens. Sam saw two state troopers speed past the van and come to a screeching halt on the side of the road up the embankment from where he stood. Troopers piled out of their vehicles, guns drawn.

"Freeze," the young highway patrol man said to Sam as he walked out from the cornfield into the beam of the Trooper's take down light.

"Take it easy. I'm frozen," Sam said in reply.

"On the ground!"

Just as Sam was getting to the ground, he said "I'm a cop, hold your fire."

Another voice said, "A cop maybe, a menace for sure!"

"That you, Don?" Sam said from the dirt.

"Now why am I not surprised it's you, Sam? Come on up. Trooper, lower your weapon before it accidentally goes off and we have the whole Masai nation down on us!" a bemused trooper called out as he got out of his vehicle.

Bewildered, the trooper followed his superior's order and holstered his sidearm.

Sam limped a little up the hill and walked over to Lt. Donald Brown and shook his hand.

"What the hell happened? Automatic gunfire on my stretch of highway?"

"What can I say, Don? Somebody doesn't like me."

"Lots of people don't like you. Fortunately, they're mostly bad guys."

Brown's shoulder mike squawked and a voice reported that a dead body had been found at the convenience store.

"Buddy of yours?" Brown quipped.

"Tried to play Doctor with me and didn't want to play nice."

Sam caught a ride back with Brown as his car was towed to the nearest impound lot. It was evidence after all, and Sam didn't care too much. He wouldn't be driving that vehicle again anyway. Brown dropped him off at a rental agency where he rented a new Corvette.

Walker had given him permission to see what the Vette 'could do'. He alerted the troopers on the way back to Patience to let Sam pass, no matter how fast he was going. Walker owed Sam more than he could ever repay, he thought as he idly touched the place on his arm where the small Special Forces tattoo was.

Sam flew the Vette back to Patience and was there in half the time. He went directly to the bunker and straight to the back room where he picked up the phone and called his father. He quickly gave his account of what had happened, and he could tell from his father's tone that he expected the situation to escalate. It was time to get ready.

CHAPTER
SEVENTEEN

"We have to celebrate our victory, Virgil!"

"What did we do?" Virgil asked in complete bewilderment.

"We cracked it! We know some of the products. Our data has gotten results," Doc said.

"I knew it would. Them Ruskies can't mess with us good ole boys!" Virgil said.

"I know a place; let's get a drink and wind down."

"Now you're talking"

By the time the evening was over, Doc had put enough Rohypnol into Virgil's drinks that he wouldn't remember a thing. That, plus the fact that once Virgil was sufficiently oiled up they made their way to a strip bar. By the time Doc had spent a few twenties on lap dances for Virgil, with the generous assistance of a couple of the girls; a few decent lewd acts had been recorded on film.

Carlos decided that he needed to personally follow up on the botched attempt to kill Sheriff Trunce. Jose would be of no use as his new preoccupation was now stockpiling guns. At least the fool had rented an old warehouse and wasn't handling weapons at the Ramada. Besides, Carlos thought as he drove in the direction of Patience, he could call Manny the Farmer without any prying ears.

Carlos had been around enough law enforcement to know whether he was dealing with a local ticket writer or a professional. So far the home team was winning by leaps and bounds, but Manny knew a few professionals killers too, and it was time to up the ante. The last thing he wanted to do was to continue to lose men. I can explain most mistakes away, but dead associates just didn't look good, Carlos thought.

Manny the Farmer sat in the sun on his veranda, watching his workers out in the Agave fields nearest to his home. He grew the plants that made the real tequila and provided him with status and as cover for his other operations. He was dressed in comfortable work clothes for traveling around the Hacienda, which he did every day. He treated his men well and they worshiped him. He paid better than most and took care of family problems, sick children, did all of the things that made life a little easier in rural Mexico. A recent convert to the cell phone, he liked knowing that the phone was not tied to him or his legitimate businesses, only his illegal operations that largely had to do with providing substances to stupid gringos who in turn provided him with cash. The fact that the gringo working class was damaged simply made it easier for Mexicans in search of better jobs and homes in America. Manny was fiercely patriotic and felt that it was about time for the migrant Mexican worker to get their own back, after decades of abuse by American companies and exploitation by the border patrol. Years ago as a young man Manny had made those trips. He was a quick learner. Combined with his ruthless and cunning nature, he had pulled himself and his family up from poverty to a position of respect and power. As he gazed out at the Agave, one of the cell phones on the table in front of him rang.

"It is Carlos."

"Good to hear from you Carlos. What news?"

"I have filed a summary at the usual location. It bears attention."

"I will give it my utmost attention. I appreciate the information."

Manny turned off the phone. He would have preferred an oral report but he knew he could access a web posting so remote that it could never be traced back to him. He had sent a few of the brighter sons and daughters of the men he employed off to earn degrees to assist in their work for him. All business was handled as business and this report would be presented to him and then appropriately disposed of.

"Manolo, please print out the report from the Midwest. I would like to review it."

A slender bookish man quickly left the room. Minutes later he returned with the report, handing it to Manny.

Manny slid on his glasses and began to read the document, with a growing sense of disbelief. Unlike his nephew, he had never been hotheaded. He thought things out. He didn't always make the right decision, but he did not act rashly. He shook his head as he read the report. He had wondered how long it would be before a community fought back directly. In Mexico, things were handled on a much more immediate and local basis. America was different and that was one of the things that made it easier to do business there.

He took off his glasses and thought of his retreat in Cuba, which was also his escape route if anything ever went wrong. His wife was now deceased and his children were provided for with foreign trust funds. They had no knowledge that he was anything other than a successful merchant farmer. Two of the men who had died in the minivan were from the Hacienda and were assuredly following his nephew's directives. There would have to be consequences for their deaths, but then he would be done with Jose and tell his sister he was just out of the business, and that her precious son was ready to go out on his own. While he was angry with Jose for forcing his hand, Manny wasn't disappointed at the prospect of retirement.

Manny picked up his own land phone and placed a call. It was time to make the necessary arrangements. A meeting was called for. He would also arrange for a flight to Cuba. He wanted to visit his friend Fidel and get the house ready. It was time for a permanent vacation. Unfortunately, there was first retribution to consider. He felt he owed his men that. Their families would be provided for, and he intended to leave the Hacienda in the capable hands of his management; they ran it anyway.

Paco Daga turned the old jeep down the dusty road and headed to the Hacienda. Manny had called him for a conference, which was extraordinary. He spoke with the Patron often, but in the field and usually about the crop and farm matters. Once in a while the Patron asked his advice when bloodshed was imminent. In his old life, he had experience with that. Paco was not Mexican. He was Cuban and a hero of the revolution. He wasn't an idealist; he just knew how bad it had been under Batista. Fidel's Cuba was better in most ways, but its continued communism hurt the people now that the USSR had fallen. The ongoing US embargo was just wrong, especially in light of the fact that every other western nation had reestablished trade with Cuba. The United States was a huge source of tourism and capital, crucial investment that the country needed.

As he drove, Paco remembered his time fighting in the hills of his beloved Cuba and the heady days of revolution. He had gone on to train soldiers and unofficially fight in other struggles following orders from his superiors. He remembered training the Viet Cong and fighting alongside them in clandestine battles, finally enjoying victory. He had never tasted defeat. He had felt a sense of betrayal when the USSR dissolved and left his country adrift. His former Russian masters had trained him well. He had been as elite as any soldier of his day. He retired and was forgotten, and that was fine with him. He'd never taken a wife, but had family to visit, as he did on his trips to Cuba. He had a position of honor and trust with the Patron, and learned to love the land and farming. After so much destruction and death his life was now about life and the men he now led in a struggle against nature to bring in the crop.

He stopped the car in the circular drive of the Hacienda and stepped out into the front yard, which was really more of a garden. He admired the home and was proud that the Patron was not an ostentatious, wasteful man. The home was beautiful, but not unnecessarily grand. The natural beauty of the area, with its high plateaus and extinct volcano, was just part of the magic of the Agave liquor they distilled there.

Manny stepped out of the front door and walked over to Paco.

"Como Estas, Patron?"

"We are old men Paco. I always ask you to call me Manny."

"I forget, sir, too many years taking command."

"That is what I need your advice on my old friend. Let's have a drink and refresh ourselves."

Manny led Paco to a table in a cool spot in the front garden and the two men sat in comfortable chairs around a stone table in the shade. A couple of iguanas languished nearby and eyed them.

Manny poured a couple of glasses of his best reserve 100 proof Agaves. He handed the small Caballito glass to Paco and left him to serve himself some of the Sangrita mixture of tomato and orange juice, salt and chili.

Manny poured himself a glass and explained the situation in Patience to Paco. He spoke directly and provided the report that he had earlier reviewed. Once he had finished he explained his plan.

"Paco, I wish you to select a squad of your choice from among the men, of whatever number you think appropriate. These men and you will travel to this town and retaliate. Call it revenge if you must, but it will be done, the deputies as well, but only combatants, no children. I think that this is the work of a small number, but the weaponry used is troubling. Not only that they possess it, but that they used it and there was no report or action of any kind taken by law enforcement. They are either lucky amateurs or professionals. I do not believe in luck. My nephew will be instructed to follow your lead. Use him and his men as you think it best. You have complete discretion to decide how to proceed. My nephew is at best a loose cannon, but he can be controlled. I will be leaving once you are on the ground in Missouri. I must leave on a strong note, not only for myself, but for the good of the families."

Paco listened quietly and began to formulate a list of men in his mind. He never questioned the motives or activities of the Patron's business. He suspected drugs, but as long as it hurt his country's oppressors, the activity had its merit. That was enough for him. He would do the job and return to quietly live out his life, working in the sun, relaxing in the shade and sipping the fruit of his labors.

"It will be done, Patron."

"What of your fields, Paco?" Manny asked as the men enjoyed their drinks and drifted onto more pleasant subjects.

CHAPTER
EIGHTEEN

Sam starred into the campfire, going over the recent attack in his mind. To his right, his father sat forward to speak.

"We could really use some more intel on this one, boys. I don't like flying blind," John said placing another log into the fire pit on Nathan's deck and poking it into place with a long iron rod sending sparks up into the night sky.

"It could be anything. It's not that hard to get fully automatic weapons these days. It doesn't necessarily mean that we're dealing with anything more sophisticated than some street gang used to shooting first and asking questions later," Sam said quietly, the glow of the fire reflecting the concern on his face.

"True, but we can't really ask them any questions, since they're in little pieces all over the corn field," Nathan said patting John Trunce on the back.

"We'll plan for the worst. In my experience it's those situations where you make broad assumptions that tend to blow up in your face. I've seen the ferocity and expert execution that 'simple villagers' are capable of with some well-organized direction," John continued.

"This is also a Mexican outfit, undoubtedly connected to organized crime in that country. They have been known to send a message by coming after family. We need to be ready for that," Sam added.

"I'll contact each person to get schedules and determine if any additional weapons are necessary. I think we should have two headquarters, the bunker and the ridge behind Sam's house. Each person will be assigned a fallback position nearest to their homes," John said.

"We can dig in on the ridge. I agree we need to draw any fireworks as far from the town as possible. The last thing I want is a bunch of yahoos from the tavern trying to help us by running around with shotguns and .22s," Sam said.

"The ridge is fortified," John said simply.

"So that's what you do with your spare time Dad. I assume it's provisioned as well?"

"Not the yummiest food ever, but I've got water, ammo, and communications gear."

Sam smiled at the old warrior; one more time into the breach. It had been a long time since John Trunce had been in combat, but it was what he did best. He still trained as if a call to war was only around the corner. I suppose, Sam thought, that if you'd been called three times to big ones and who knows how many times to other operations, the call is just around the corner. It did not matter to Sam that John was pushing eighty years old. His mind was sharp and he was as deadly as ever, he'd shown that. Sam pitied anyone who went up against him and was glad to have him. They would be ready.

"Nathan, please call and tell your father I need him," John said.

Nathan smiled and said, "He has been preparing also and waiting for your orders."

"He is the best soldier I've ever known, you know."

"He says the same thing of you, and that you taught him everything he knows about war."

John smiled and was transported more than thirty years back in time to a dark jungle, trapped in an ambush by an unknown number of the enemy, alone with his executive officer, fighting for their lives. They should have both been dead and they knew it. They had escaped by diving down a ravine, something that only a crazy person would attempt. Neither man had to talk the other into it, they just went. It was a day for miracles, and every day since, combat or no, had been gravy.

Joseph Harper sat in his kitchen and watched as his wife sharpened a stabbing spear in a methodical and intensely frightening way. He marveled once again that an old farm boy from Mississippi had pursued and won an African princess. She was as dark as night, lean and spare. Her body had no fat. She worked hard with her husband and son, living largely off the land. She took great pride in her life and could never understand why anyone would need to go to a gym. She would smile and say, "Dance more." Harper had learned to love the life outside, from his years in the Masai camp and raising his son in the Missouri woods. His wife never complained. He had learned to read her, and knew when it was time to hop on a plane and go to Africa. She was the most spontaneous woman he had ever known. He had learned that planning was overrated and that being able to adapt was part of life. More than once he had taken her hand and led her to the car, driven to the airport, and jumped on a plane. Once Nathan had gotten older he just took care of their livestock and farm when his father asked him.

She looked up at her husband, smiled, and continued to sharpen the wicked looking spear. "The dogs who come for us will know we are Masai."

No shit, Harper thought as he watched her, a princess of an ancient nation of pure warriors. No long distance anything. You looked your enemy in the eye when you killed him and he looked you in the eye when he tried to kill you. The Masai saw a beauty in that brutality. They always seemed anxious to get to it, and that was as scary as hell. Ua, he thought, a lovely name. What most people didn't know was that in Swahili his wife's name meant flower. It also meant kill. Joseph, remembering his history, recalled that when the British tried to colonize that area of Africa, now Kenya, they wisely went around the Masai.

CHAPTER
NINETEEN

Virgil woke up with the worst hangover ever. He was lying in a cornfield next to his house. He didn't even have the luxury of knowing what he's done to end up that way. His head felt like an anvil, his stomach like a sewer. He was a nervous shaky wreck and now he had to go in and face his wife.

As he stood he thought, Oh just take me now Lord. He ambled over to the front door and tried the knob, and found it locked. Not good. He saw the wall clock through the kitchen window; it was ten to five in the morning. He never came home that late. Virgil reached into his pocket to see if by some miracle his keys were still in his pocket. He pulled out his keys and some snap shots. Holy shit. And what the damn hell? Strippers? His reaction was mixed; a little upset he couldn't remember any of it, but mostly abject horror. These we burn, and right now. Virgil walked over to his burn barrel and destroyed the evidence. He began to formulate a plan, the old 'ran into an old buddy routine.' This time when he got to the door, Martha his wife was there, waiting for him. To his surprise she hugged and kissed him, put him in a shower, and put him to bed. No fireworks, no yelling, no questions. If he ever had to answer any questions on this one he would sure as hell hold his water on anything he knew, but as it was, he couldn't remember a damn thing. Who knew, maybe he was abducted by aliens. There had to be more than one husband or boyfriend out there who had played that card before. At least if he had been abducted it didn't feel like the aliens had probed him. That would have been just too much. Man, he felt like boiled shit.

"Virgil, you were not abducted by aliens," Sam said into the phone, glad to hear Virgil's voice. At least the mysterious abduction had been resolved.

"Well, I have no idea what happened or where I went."

"Nothing? Even when a guy drinks too much he has a clue where he started out," Sam said.

"I went up to the sawmill near the house," Virgil said.

"The meth lab, Virgil."

"The what?"

"Your abduction was more like someone slipped you a mickey, drugs to make you forget."

"They did the trick."

"Let me know if you remember anything else."

"Sam, can we not say anything to Martha?"

"That would be just too cruel, Virgil. Besides, I don't want any discussion about drug dealers in Patience. I will take care of those bastards. They are starting to piss me off. If anyone is going to knock somebody out in my county, it's going to be me!"

The more Sam thought about the Virgil situation the more he worried. Well, at least they're not butchers, but they were able to pull that off pretty easily, and that means they are at least somewhat sophisticated. They understood that dead bodies complicated things and sent messages instead. Anything was possible. Leaving Virgil alive had been a tactical move. Dead bodies put people on alert, and gave them a chance to prepare. If the enemy had any plans for retaliation, they wouldn't want anyone prepared. An old, raw feeling started in Sam's belly. He had seen his share of clandestine combat missions. There always seemed to be some kind of 'calm before the storm'. He didn't think it would be long before everything went to hell.

CHAPTER
TWENTY

Tracy Trunce sat in his office at NSA headquarters and reviewed a report that noted several intercepted reports going to and from Manny the Farmer, an individual who the DEA suspected had some involvement in drug trafficking into the US, but that was it. They had no proof, and the communications were in a code that so far the cryptographers and their massive array of computers could not crack. They knew that it was military, and Tracy did not like that at all. He wanted to find out what kind of network, if any, his brother was up against, not only from a local perspective but from a global one. Tracy knew how little incidents could become big ones. He picked up the phone and called Patience.

"Hello Tracy," Moon said as he sat in an office tucked far back at the bunker that served as Sam's sheriff station. He adjusted his lab coat over his slender frame and leaned back in his chair.

"How did you know it was me?"

"Very few people use this line. I like it like that. It's kind of like the Bat phone."

"Moon, while you're manning the bat cave, I need you to do some research on a guy named, Manny the Farmer. He is a bad guy from Mexico who might have some resources in Missouri to harass certain elements of regional law enforcement efforts."

"I see. Do you have a triangulation point?" Moon said.

"I have a source server, but who knows where the actual origin is," Tracy said.

"Send me what you've got, I'll go hunting."

Sam drove an old four door sedan down a street in East St. Louis, trying not to look too white. The car was a beater and wouldn't attract any significant notice. It was like the old Sex Pistol's lyric, "I look around your house, you've got nothing to steal." He just needed a quick in and out. The man he needed to get a message to didn't take calls, and sure as hell didn't spend much time traveling the countryside. Sam pulled into the small parking lot of a southern-style rib joint. It was mid-afternoon, so there were only a few faces around, customers loafing around in the front of the store. The tables were old and bolted to the floor. Everything had that well-used but still useful look. There was a short menu on the wall and you could get cans of beer and soda. No bottles; best not to hand out weapons in a downright dangerous place like East St. Louis.

Sam walked into the restaurant in beat up jeans and a fraying old t-shirt, looking very un-cop like. He walked up to the counter and said, "Elmore in back?"

"Elmore," the old man behind the counter yelled instantly, "lost white man to see you."

"Fuck 'em," came back a snarly retort.

"He don't have that 'I think I'd like to get fucked by a scraggly old black man look to him." Although Sam didn't look like a cop, he looked like he could handle himself, and without a doubt had guns on him. Both assessments were correct.

"Well God damn, I'm cooking! Everybody thinks this meat falls from the damn trees! This ain't no squirt some shit on a backyard grill and burn the shit out of everything deal here, I got food on!"

"You always got food on you mangy old picker!" Sam yelled.

A rangy old rail of a man came hurrying out of the back. He had a smile that few people got to see on a regular basis, but he always had it for Sam.

"Elmore Whitman Smith, BBQ king," Sam yelled.

The older man rushed over and clasped Sam's hand and clapped him on the back.

"Bad ass Sam Trunce," he left out the crazy cop part. It just was not the place for it.

"Sit down, Sam. Iced tea?"

"Absolutely, but can I see the smokehouse?"

Another huge beam from Smith. "Sure, come on back. I'll always show you what's cookin.'"

"Now I've heard you say that to the ladies back at Detroit Charlie's a time or to."

"God don't mention that place. We both got out just in time, you with your ass, and me with my guitar and BBQ recipe and not much else. I ain't never going any farther back up north than I am right now, never!"

Sam just nodded and put his hand on Smith's bony shoulder. Sam had helped Smith's grandson, saved his life in the very shootout that had almost taken Sam. When it was over, all the bad guys were dead and Sam lived. Smith had never heard of so many dead people in one room. Smith thought Sam was nothing short of the toughest man he'd ever heard of. Smith had rarely played his guitar in front of white people until he did it in Detroit as part of a blues band that got gigs in nice places. He had a following. Real blues people knew who Elmore Whitman Smith was. His guitar made you cry, but not so bad that you couldn't eat his BBQ.

"Well son, I know you didn't come down here to say howdy. What's up?"

"My dad wants to talk to Junior."

"He may be my employer, but he's also almost as bad an ass as you, and definitely don't wear no white hat."

"Dad needs a favor."

Smith remembered how Sam's father had got him this job when they left Detroit. One day they drove to this very BBQ joint, and that old ranger had asked the same old man out front to see Sgt. Junior Williams. How deferential the obvious gangster had been to the old man; great respect was shared. Junior himself had gotten an apron from the back for Smith and said simply, "If he can cook fine. If he can't cook fine, but he has a job until I say he don't have a job."

Smith fondly remembered how they all had reacted when they tried his BBQ. Like all really good cooks, he knew his food was good. People didn't have to say it, but it didn't hurt. That was more than four years ago, and more than a few real blues gigs. He got to do both things he loved again, after he thought he'd lose it all. There's no joy in living the blues, life just works that way a lot.

"I will tell him right away. I know he will call your dad. Everything okay with you, Sam?"

"Me, I'm fine, just a Mexican meth problem."

"Those drug problems don't always turn out so good," Smith gave Sam a knowing look.

"I know it, but this time they're on my turf and have my friends to deal with."

Sam and Smith ate some BBQ and Smith sent Sam home with his sauce. Sam knew if he asked he'd get the recipe, but knew better than to ask.

CHAPTER
TWENTY-ONE

Behind the barn, a dilapidated storm cellar door hid a flight of cement steps. At the bottom, an electronic keypad guarded a heavy steel door. Very few people knew of the room behind the barn, and only a few had been inside.

The room and its contents gave John Trunce a sense of attachment to his old profession, as well as a sense of security. Behind the security door were racks of weapons and ammunition. Despite his eighty years, every gun was clean, oiled and ready for use. From here he had seen too many wars and too much combat to think that attack was impossible within the United States. 9-11 had also shown that to be not only possible, but probable now. He hadn't been surprised in the least, only by the fact that it hadn't occurred earlier. John thought of the people, who lived in all of the places where he'd fought, and how war was thrust upon them. How the peace and order of their lives had been shattered for years and in some cases decades by war. John knew the United States wasn't immune. This situation was no different in his mind. It was an attack on the lives and safety of his friends and neighbors. It was chemical warfare, just delivered a little differently. If there was to be retaliation against his family, friends, and community, it would be met with a more than determined resistance. If he could, he personally would kill them all. That was flat it. John did not have to remind himself that he was good at war. He was a living encyclopedia of modern combat knowledge and experience. He didn't give a damn that he was pushing eighty years old. He remembered that many of the village elders who worked with the Viet Cong in Vietnam would have been considered old, but they fought alongside the men, women, and children against the world's best equipped army and won. John also knew that the people he could count on if the fight came to them also felt as he did. These were people who lived as they did because of the experiences that they had lived through, so that they could find a small corner of the world and live in peace. Life to them was not about how much you can get, but how well you can live. They had all seen the abomination that the accumulation of wealth and power can become. War was never really about ideology, it was about power. Nothing had changed. Ideology was the mask leaders used to motivate the masses. A way to control people and to get them to go to war and fight, or to strap bombs to themselves and kill innocents.

John turned on the light and the room was illuminated. Racks of weapons were on the walls, each with a chest of ammunition beneath it. There were several automatic weapons, some modern and some dated, but all fully operational. John had two sixty caliber machine guns on tripods and thousands of rounds of ammunition. There were Claymore mines, rocket launchers, grenades and other manner of explosives: weapons from all of the wars he'd seen. John selected several lighter machine guns and ammo, carried them up into the main area of the barn and wrapped each in oil cloth and placed them in cases for transport. He took several grenades and cased those also. These were more modern, and he didn't want any mistakes. He and Moon had reworked all of the explosive ordinance as it had come into his possession. There could be no mistakes when it came to them.

John pulled his jeep alongside the table where all of the cases were set, loaded them into the back seat and covered them with a tarp and strapped them down.

"John, do you think it will come to needing all that?" He looked up. Karen was standing in the doorway with a worried look on her face.

"I hope not, but I don't know. I can tell you that we will all be prepared if it happens. It will be what it will be. Nobody will leave, you know that. Maybe this is just our time. I don't understand much of anything about drugs and the like, but that doesn't matter. We have to draw the line, and it might as well start here."

"I know you are right and I'm glad you're here."

"I am glad to be here, with Karen Trunce and her Winchester."

Karen smiled and hugged John, "The crazy thing about being older is that you worry a little less about dying, don't you John? We've lived a long time and been very lucky. I just don't want to go out feeling useless."

"There's little chance of that."

"Where will I be?" Karen asked.

"Where do you want to be?"

"With you, but I know that won't work."

John smiled and brushed her cheek, "Now you know how you tend to distract me," he said with a sly grin and meaningful voice.

"You bad man, John Trunce."

"Card carrying," he said. They both knew that for John to function he couldn't be worrying about her, as he would if she was with him.

"I'll go and stay with Madeleine. I doubt there will be trouble there. Besides, I pity anyone who takes on Madeleine Toche, especially in her own home."

"More importantly, in her own restaurant," John said.

They both smiled as Karen said, "The French and their food."

John kissed Karen and drove down a dirt trail behind his home and up along the ridge that separated his land from the valley, where the creek and the next ridge that led down to the outskirts of town and Madeleine's restaurant were. It was 2:30, a good time to be stopping by. Lunch was over and Madeleine would be expecting him.

He pulled up behind the restaurant and Madeleine came out with a dish towel over her shoulder and walked to the jeep.

"Bonjour John, I see you have brought friends to keep me company."

"Of course, Madeleine. May I show them inside?"

"This way."

John picked up one of the smaller cases and carried it into the back door of the building and down the stairs to the cellar. Madeleine led the way and turned on the light. John opened the case and took out two small bundles and two small ammo boxes. Madeleine picked up one of the bundles and unwrapped the cloth. When she saw what was inside she whistled, "I haven't seen one of these since the war. You are thoughtful to provide me with something with which I am all too familiar." Deftly she inspected the weapon, expertly breaking it down and reassembling it.

"The Germans did many things well. The MP 40 is one of them," John said.

"I carried and used one for years. It is reliable and sturdy," She said dispassionately as if describing a vacuum cleaner.

"There are two for your convenience and a thousand rounds."

Madeleine opened both ammo boxes and in the second were two grenades. She looked at John and didn't say anything. She just closed the boxes and moved to a corner of the room where she temporarily locked them in a sturdy trunk.

"Thank you John. I think we should have some wine, and you can tell me what you know," she said as they walked back up the concrete steps to the kitchen above.

CHAPTER
TWENTY-
TWO

S am sat in Nathan's kitchen with Nathan, his mother, and father. "Dad will come by with whatever you need."

"He's already been and we're ready, Sam. We've already planned to head to the ridge once the shit hits the fan." Unlike John, Joseph didn't even try to suggest to Nathan and Ua that they would be better off with anyone other than himself. It would have been a bad idea, and the anger it would have caused would have been legendary. Both Nathan and his mother knew how to fire all of the weapons at their disposal if necessary. Nathan would be mobile, and the ridge was his Alamo.

Paco stood before a group of men who functioned as the Hacienda's foremen, under the shade of an awning that briefly protected them from the unrelenting desert sun that beat down. They were also all completely loyal to their Patron, each with a story of survival and aid from the man.

"Men, I am putting a team of soldiers together to carry out a mission for our Patron. I need you to discretely inquire among the men under your authority to find those who have prior military experience, and then simply send them to me. Marco and Philippe have served with me in the past," Paco said as he gestured to two of the men in the group. "They will evaluate others who may not have prior experience but have the necessary characteristics for the job. I know that all of the men would fight and die for the Patron, and he appreciates that sacrifice, but prior training is essential to the successful completion of this task. Please do this immediately, and in three days we will begin to choose the men."

After dismissing the men, Paco directed Marco and Philippe over to a table that was positioned under the awning. Once they sat he unrolled a couple of maps that were set over to the side.

"This will be a slash and burn mission, strictly to send a message and to even the score for our men. We have no idea of what we will find, whether it is one rogue sheriff or a group of vigilantes. One thing we do know is that they are well armed. The Patron is a cautious man, as am I, and we will go in prepared. Our man on the ground will assess the situation and determine what the enemy's strength is. The Patron's nephew is his representative in the area and will be of whatever assistance I determine."

Both men smiled very slightly and made eye contact with Paco. They were his men from his days with the Cuban Army. He trusted them completely, but they both knew that meaningful glances were much less likely to land them in trouble than any open commentary on the idiocy of the man under discussion. They remembered well the Patron's attempts to educate his nephew concerning Agaves farming and their disastrous results. The nephew had basically spent his days harassing the daughters of the men, smoking cigars and driving over equipment and buildings when he had sampled too much farm produce. They excused all of it in deference to their Patron, and because the nephew was indeed loyal to his uncle. Manny seemed to have a gift for that: people just didn't want to disappoint him.

"We will be crossing the desert into Arizona. We will travel light and use those days to finish our training. I agree with the Patron that we must not only be prepared, but also patient. If the Enemy expects or is preparing for an attack; they will expect it to be swift. The longer we wait, within reason, the less and less the enemy will expect us to retaliate. We will train hard, starting now. We will train with the men."

"Weapons, Jeffe?" Marco, the taller, leaner man, said in a quiet voice.

Paco regarded the man and his memory went back to a jungle a long time ago, and how Marco was so cool in combat, detached and machine like. He was as dependable as the sun that beat down outside the awning, and just as deadly.

"The Patron will provide what we need. I have compiled a list. If you feel there are other things that we need just say so."

Both men looked at the list, which included a small arsenal of automatic weapons, RPGs, explosives, and high tech gear. Based on the list they immediately reassessed the situation.

"We are going into formal combat." It wasn't a question from Philippe, just a statement of fact.

Paco smiled at him, it was hard not to. He was a true comrade in arms. Every bit as reliable as Marco, he was the opposite in every way. Even when things were their worst and morale was the lowest, Philippe would joke or cajole with the men. Both men commanded respect, Marco more through quiet intimidation. The men loved Philippe. It was always obvious that their safety was his first concern. A man would rather be put through physical hell than lose his respect. He now worked alongside his men in peace the way he did in war.

"We will begin to train in two days, both physical and weapons training. We will need to train for house to house and wilderness. We are going to Missouri, USA. The woods are not as dense as jungle, but provide their own set of problems."

"Snakes, Jeffe?" Philippe asked.

"Some, and they don't rattle," Paco responded.

The men laughed. Men who worked outside in arid desert-like conditions most of the time usually carried small caliber pistols for snakes.

"I was more worried about how they tasted, Heffe. You know, fried up with a little salt and lime?"

Carlos sat at a table at a family restaurant just outside of St. Louis and spoke to a middle aged man across from him who was probably the most forgettable looking individual he had ever seen. His name was Smith, no first name. He was neither tall, nor short, nor heavy, nor thin. From time to time the organization would call in his services for gathering information when it was best not to arouse suspicion. He certainly did not look Hispanic at all. He looked Midwestern normal. He was medium height medium weight. He sat motionlessly wearing a baseball cap with the visor pulled down. He had no scars, no moles, no smile and no personality.

"I need recon on this man," Carlos slid over a picture of Sam Trunce. The man looked at it but made no effort to pick it up. "I need to know his habits, where he goes and what he does and who he cares for. Take no action. Go in with cover and don't be discovered."

Abruptly the conversation was over and Smith got up and left the table, moving silently. None of the other diners looked up. It never ceased to amaze Carlos that Smith could participate in a conversation without speaking. As usual, he had taken an assignment without uttering a word. Creepy, but it made sense. Carlos would receive a report posted in code on an obscure message board in a few days. It would be complete, both tactically and otherwise. The man had other talents, and perhaps this whole matter would still be solved with the accidental death of one sheriff, nice and quiet.

Smith left the restaurant and crossed a parking lot in front of a large chain grocery store. He removed his false mustache and wig and popped out two contacts that changed the color of his eyes. He knew his business. He did not like to kill, nor did he have any specific political affiliation. He simply carried out what he had been trained to do against targets who had involved themselves one way or another in a dangerous game. Sometimes the targets were political, military, or law enforcement, other times, private individuals. He did not kill women or children, except collaterally and only under extreme circumstances. He did not make mistakes. He could make the trip quite easily, and with the aid of a small digital camera, get all of the information he needed. The pay was good and this wasn't a hit, at least not yet. But his intelligence gathering skills allowed him to assess from both a strategic assassination perspective and a combat one. He would do both.

CHAPTER
TWENTY-
THREE

In a dusty brown sedan of indeterminate pedigree, Smith drove past the worn 'Welcome to Patience' sign and down the town's main strip. Nothing unusual about this place, he thought. Looks like small town main street USA wherever you go. He drove past a bank on the corner and saw a medium sized grocery store and pulled into the parking lot. On these types of recon missions, he liked to pick up a couple of bags of groceries. Besides, he needed a couple of chew bones for the old beagle spread over the back seat. In his mind, a man walking a dog was about the best cover you can get, especially an old, half blind, couch lump like Cochise. The dog was about as unlike his fierce warrior namesake as a dog could be. He'd buy a nice steak and some charcoal and grill in the park by the river he saw next to the small motel he had passed on the way into town. Just passing through. He mused that his conduct might seem awfully domestic to the men and governments that hired him to kill people, but that was his job, not his life. He didn't have an immediate family of his own, just a brother and sister, both on the west coast, and some extended family. They thought he was in insurance. In a way he was.

As he exited the grocery he saw a squad car rolling by, driven by a largish man with dirty blond hair and ray ban sunglasses on. He immediately identified the driver as the primary target of his surveillance. Without rushing he put the groceries in the back seat with the dog and pulled out onto the street and followed the squad, keeping it a few blocks ahead. The squad pulled into the parking lot of what had to be the sheriff's station. What the building lacked in ugly it made up for in sheer intimidation quality. He had seen bomb shelters that looked like quaint cabins compared to this thing. He fully expected to see rifle ports in the side of the walls and crenellations in the entryway for the defenders to rain boiling oil down on their enemies. He did not like what he saw. Whoever built that thing was a man who held his ground and was prepared to fight back. He noted a couple other squads there and made mental notes about troop strength. For him it was automatic, from years of training and legitimate government missions, at least sanctioned by the government at some level. Given that it was later in the afternoon, he parked his car a couple of blocks from the station and hooked the dog to a leash and walked and waited. His hunch was correct: it had been a whistle stop by the man to check on things, another indication of competence. It may have been routine, but adhering to routine, especially for security reasons, meant the man was diligent and observant. A picture of his adversary started to form in the man's mind.

He put the dog back in the car and followed the squad at a discrete distance to a large house on the outskirts of town. To his surprise it was a restaurant. He changed his dinner plans, cracked the window for the dog and went inside. He was seated at a small table near a side window with a view of the river that meandered by. He was immediately struck by the quality of the smells that permeated the dining area. No wonder the man came here. If it tasted as good as it smelled he was in for a treat. So far on this job he had broken no laws, and he intended to act as such and allow himself a little pleasure. As he looked over the menu, he noticed the man sitting with an older woman, a young boy and a strikingly beautiful woman in her early thirties. They conversed and laughed with ease, and he could tell at this distance that there was chemistry between the man and the dark and beautiful woman who sat quite close to him. Smith enjoyed his meal. He had a fine vegetable soup with as delicate a broth as he had ever eaten, followed by a piece of trout that tasted like it had just swum onto his plate along with a sprinkling of butter and fine herbs. The main course was Daube served in a small ceramic pot with a lid. He had a salad with vinaigrette and selected two cheeses from a cart his waitress brought to the table, a goat cheese and a piece of Monbriac, which he was shocked to find here in the Missouri sticks. He had a half carafe of the house red. It had to be a Cote Du Rhone or something similar. This place was a gem. Then he caught in the distance, presumably on the way into the kitchen, an exchange of French, and it all made sense.

During his meal his target left, but he had done enough surveillance for the day. One mistake that amateurs made was to rush a job and attract attention. He had learned to tailor the action to the situation, and at present there was no urgency.

Sam had that prickly feeling that somebody was watching him but he couldn't see any evidence of it. It hadn't spoiled his time with Christine or her son. He had been making excuses to go to the restaurant, and she seemed to be mysteriously running into him around town. He had just suggested a fishing excursion after the boy went back in the kitchen. Christine had accepted and in broken English, said that she would pack a lunch for two. He couldn't have been happier. The kid was great, but he thought it was time to see if there were any sparks. All the signs were there. He felt very different about this relationship. It consumed his thoughts, and while he had had other relationships in the past, they lacked any depth, at least from his side. His heart had been in some, but those times it was much more like he had followed a path that he felt he was expected to. Maybe his standards were high or he valued his freedom. Everything was out the window here. It was funny the way that his friends and family looked at the two of them. It was if they saw something he couldn't see. To Sam it seemed that everything was a little brighter, and his problems were less important. He wondered about the potential for retaliation from the Meth boys as the days went by, but he followed his father's advice. Not everyone who seeks revenge is a wild idiot. It is the act of revenge, not when it happens, that's important. The best example was when the unborn son of a murdered father grows up and kills the murderer. Sam didn't want the waiting to go on forever, and knew that with Tracy pushing from his end either the battle would come to them, or he would take the battle wherever it needed to go. Drug wars among the Mexican gangs were rampant, and he had no compunction about joining them for a few days. He also expected to hear from the East St. Louis connection soon. There was going to be a fight somewhere.

CHAPTER
TWENTY-
FOUR

Junior Carter drove a borrowed pickup truck down the highway, through Patience and toward John Trunce's home. He had been there on a couple of occasions when it had been best for him to be outside of St. Louis. His old commander never asked any questions and trusted that if Junior had done any killing, it had been of somebody that needed killing. By definition, cops, women, kids, and civilians did not need killing, as John had casually mentioned once upon a time. That was fine with Junior. Killing was costly; it made people uncomfortable, and that was bad for business. It was more the threat of it that kept people in line, except when other killers try to run you and your killers out of a territory, that's different. Junior wasn't much for the drug end of things, but you couldn't have drug dealers moving into your area. He made his money the old fashioned way: numbers, hookers, theft, and protection here and there. All tried and true and what people wanted, and generally, fairly peaceful.

Junior pulled his hat down and kept his huge mirrored sunglasses on. He didn't want to feel conspicuous in an area that had a very small black population, one that largely consisted of a giant, a Masai princess and his friend and comrade, Joseph. Junior didn't hate white people, but couldn't help mumbling, "Man, I am driving through Cracker Ville USA here."

He drove through the front gate of John Trunce's property, over a short bridge, and down a gravel road. The woods had grown even thicker since he'd been here last. He peered into the woods and brambles on either side of the road, and thought how much he wouldn't want to be the guy coming up the road to do harm. As he pulled into the courtyard area, John walked from around the side of the shed and up to his door.

"Good to see you, Colonel," Junior said.

"I appreciate your help on this one Junior. Find anything out?"

Junior held up a small manila envelope. "Got some good recon."

"Good man."

Despite himself, Junior smiled. Praise from his old commander felt better than anything had in a long time. He remembered those fearsome days in the bush. John Trunce had got him through it, which was a fact. "Karen's got some catfish and tea inside, come on in," John said.

For the next couple of hours there was no discussion about what Junior found out. John knew all of that would be in the materials. He had personally trained him and he had proven to be his best. Junior used those skills in his life on the other side of the law. He did nothing without a guaranteed outcome. Karen hugged Junior like a long lost son. Junior got a chance to feel normal and homey for a while. These people were as close to parents as he had, having grown up on the streets with parents now dead, who were unable to care for themselves, much less children. When they died, he picked up that chore for his brothers and sisters and carried it to this day.

Junior drove away and John and Karen waved. John then went behind the barn and down to his storage room to assess the materials.

In addition to wall to wall weaponry, the storage room had an office complete with computer, fax, and copiers, very much like a business office. John had done some consulting after leaving the military and used the office to keep track of that modest business. He still got many calls pleading for his services, but he felt he'd done enough. He was more interested in his corner of the world now. He would have liked grandchildren, but neither son seemed to think that a priority. Sam was a more distinct possibility, maybe even more so now, he thought as he smiled. That French girl has her sights on him, and even, despite the danger they face, Sam seemed focused and more centered than he had in some time.

He opened the packet and found a CD-Rom inside and put it into his machine. True to his word, Junior not only had live surveillance footage, there was a typed narrative also. The footage was primarily of a porky Hispanic man walking a highly energetic dog around a green area outside of an extended stay hotel. From time to time the same man would come out to talk to the dog walker, who seemed to be in some position of authority. John was an instant judge of combatants, and knew it was the second man who was the poised, confident one. He seemed to spend most of his time convincing the other man of each statement made to him. An indecisive leader was John's evaluation, but the center of authority for whatever group the men belonged to. There were good close-ups taken with a still camera. The narrative indicated that the names were unknown, but that at any given time the immediate group seemed to be comprised of about twelve persons. The narrative continued to state that the group seemed to keep a low profile and that no more than half of them actually stayed at the hotel. They rotated out of a Holiday Inn down the road. John created a file of the contents and emailed it to Moon. Moon would see that Tracy got it. The resources of the NSA would discern who the men were.

Smith spent the next couple of days trailing Sam, always just a little ways behind him. He recorded all of the stops that were regularly made and put addresses and names together. He identified family and friends, all seemingly very ordinary people in an ordinary place. He packed up his car and his dog and headed out of Patience to make contact. About halfway back to St. Louis and the airport he stayed at a budget hotel and used his laptop and an Internet connection to send his encrypted report. While the big sheriff was a concern, he seemed to lack any meaningful support. The deputies were an issue, but their shifts were staggered. Additional law enforcement was close to an hour away. If a team was necessary to subdue the sheriff, he would be isolated. A well planned assault would be necessary, but effective in his evaluation.

CHAPTER
TWENTY-
FIVE

Manny the Farmer sat in the old beat up jeep he liked to drive around the Hacienda and watched several men taking target practice and another group doing physical training. The shots were measured and precise, and the formation of men running was tight. Whatever these men were now, they were once good soldiers, he thought, professionals for a professional job. It was like anything else. You don't hire dentists to plumb your house.

From the house he could hear the bell of the telephone, and then one of his aides flagged him from the doorway. He waved to Manolo and swung around in a cloud and drove back a little fast. He liked to tear around in the old jeep.

He got to the back patio and was handed a report concerning the Patience County situation. He read the report carefully and then burned it in a small grill. The information gave him a great deal to consider. He walked back over to the jeep and went to find Paco. A second opinion is always best.

Smith made sure that he read the e-mail carefully, resubmitted it, and asked for confirmation, which was received. The nature of his employment had just changed and he would intervene directly. His status had changed. He was about to proceed with a criminal act of major proportion.

He opened his hard-sided luggage and opened a small false bottom. Inside was a small caliber pistol and a silencer. He often worked with a knife, but he was wary of the big sheriff with a gun on his hip and rocket launchers at his disposal. He'd considered some kind of accident with the sheriff's squad car, but there was something about that vehicle that wasn't kosher. The deep imprints of the tires told him immediately that it was armored and that there was serious horsepower under the hood. He decided that a quick, clean hit was the answer. The man lived alone at least most of the time. He didn't like collateral damage, but if others were there they would just be in the way. Sheriff Sam Trunce was about to have a bad day. He got into his vehicle, dressed in his usual blend-in-with-the-scenery clothing, a dark grey warm-up jacket and pants with dark, solid colored shoes. He drove his car to a previously chosen spot, left his car on a wooded lane half a mile from the Sheriff's house and approached through the woods at the back.

CHAPTER
TWENTY-SIX

Christine and Madeleine made the final preparations for the Friday evening meal at Chez-Toche. The doors opened for the first seating at 5:00 p.m. And the reservation book was full.

"Grandmere, Alan is still being difficult and won't sign the divorce papers. I don't want to wait any longer. I think I have Sam's attention, but I think he senses some reluctance on my part."

"Then what are you waiting for. Go get him. If you're frustrated with the situation just grab what you want and don't look back. It worked for me."

"But I'm still married."

"That's just on paper. You've got a real flesh and blood handsome young man right in front of you. He's good looking, hardworking and loyal. Yves likes him, what more do you want, besides, too long without a man and you'll drive yourself crazy."

"Grandmere! What a thing to say," Christine said laughing.

"I know what I'm talking about. I went so long during the war, that I think I did go a little crazy. I can tell you, it gave me one more reason to hate the Germans, if you know what I mean," Madeleine said flashing a big smile at Christine. Besides, look at the shoulders on that man!"

"Grandmere!" Christine said tossing a sprig of parsley in Madeleine's direction.

"I may be old, but I can still look. Oh look at the time and the people waiting on the porch. We better get started," Madeleine said, wiping her hands on her apron as she walked towards the front door.

Late the following afternoon, Christine drove to Sam's house to meet him for lunch and to go fishing. This was their first real time alone, she thought, and she was looking forward to it. Either he would kiss her or she would grab his ears and kiss him. No more waiting, her talk with Madeleine had convinced her.

Sam had told her he would meet her there. She pulled her vehicle into the driveway and parked on the far side of his barn, in the shade. She walked to the back of the house and went inside, as he had invited her to do so as he was going to be a little late. Sam had left the back door open for her. She walked in through the kitchen and noticed that it was neither Spartan nor cluttered. He probably could cook, although it wasn't a passion or a hobby. Sam's cat brushed up against her leg. She picked up the cat and snuggled it in her arms as she walked out into the living room area. Unlike many of the homes she'd seen in Patience, there were no animals on the walls, which was a big plus for her. She had trouble understanding why people would mount dead animals and fish on their walls. The hunting part was easy to understand when people did so for food. She herself was very fond of wild game, venison in particular. As she walked through the rooms, there was a sense of comfort and utility. The furniture was used but not worn, and a few pieces were newer, suggesting that he took pride in the appearance of his home. There were a few well-thumbed books on the coffee table, places bookmarked with scraps of paper. She seated herself in one of the comfortable chairs in the living room area and glanced through a National Geographic she found on the table.

A few minutes later she heard the loud roar of that crazy vehicle he called a car drive up the gravel driveway. She found her heart beating a little faster. Sam came through the front screen door with a small bouquet of wild flowers that he'd picked. She smiled and walked over to greet him.

"Missouri wild flowers I saw along the road," he smiled and lit up the room, dressed for fishing, but clean for a date, powerfully built, confident but filled with a gentle humor.

"Thank you Sam...pretty."

They both laughed a little over her broken English and his lack of more than a few French verbs and vocabulary.

"Nous mangeons, maintenant?" Christine said, motioning to the basket that she'd carried and set on the kitchen table.

"Oui, j'ai faim," Sam said, testing the little bit of French he'd picked up from a how to book and a CD he listened to in the squad.

Sam thought it best to start his exploration of the French language with the basics. "I'm hungry" pretty much covered his constant state of affairs. He was working on "you are beautiful" and hoped to move onto other essentials like: "do you want to spend the night?" and other important communication tools for dealing with someone as beautiful as she. Christine found plates and napkins in the kitchen, while Sam went and got an English-French, French-English dictionary that he'd purchased second hand in town. He also had a little gadget that computed French phrases from English text and vice-versa. He thought that it would be fun to use while they ate. Christine had brought a simple lunch of bread, cheese, Pate, and fruit, and a light white wine from the restaurant. Almost immediately the two were having fun naming the objects in the room and writing things to each other through the little computer. The wine sat, the food was untouched, and they were totally lost in each other. She had never felt such undivided attention from anyone. He certainly had that quality and lived in the moment. She sensed that although he wasn't shy, she was being handled with kid gloves, and that she would have to send the appropriate signals, to hell with that. She typed in, "embrassez-moi." Sam didn't wait for clarification. He put his hands on either side of her chair, gently lifted her face up to his and did what he had been waiting to do for a long time. When they broke they laughed together. Christine remembered the stairwell towards the front of the house that led upstairs. They could fish later. This was a man who cared for her, a virile, confident man. It had been a while, even longer during the weaning months of her marriage. She stood up and led Sam to the front of the house. There was no discussion. They moved as one and went up to the rooms above.

Stealth and concealment were Smith's best weapons. He carefully walked through the woods towards his target's home. When it came time to kill, he dehumanized his quarry by voiding the person from his mind. His actions became machine-like and focused.

Once he saw the home through the trees, he dropped to the ground and crawled on his belly using the natural cover and maintaining complete silence. He never varied in his preparation or planning, regardless of the difficulty of his mission. He was vigilant, expecting some form of exterior security system. He was surprised not to find any. That was a sign of over-confidence and gave him an important tactical edge.

When he reached the edge of the woods, he waited for several long minutes to ensure there was no outside activity. He noted two vehicles. He would have to assess if two kills were now necessary. He left the cover of the woods and made his way towards a main floor window that he felt gave him the best overall view of the home's main floor.

Christine and Sam lay in the big king sized bed and held one another as a rare summer breeze blew through the open window and across their bodies. They communicated without language and clung to each other as if they were afraid that if they let go, the whole thing would go away. Finally, Christine's stomach rumbled and Sam put his head on her perfect belly, cupping his ear as if listening for something inside. Laughing, they dressed haphazardly. He threw on some gym shorts, and she grabbed a pair and a loose tank top out of his drawer. He whistled, in no way teasing. She looked fantastic. Lunch wouldn't last long if he could help it. As she walked past him she playfully slapped him on the butt and trounced down the steps. Sam followed close behind. As they got to the bottom and started to cross the room, he saw something out of place. A shadow, clearly of a man by the window raising what could only be a pistol. He tackled Christine as a shot whined over his back. He scrambled and pulled her away from the shattered window. Just as he was scrambling for the gun he had hanging on the coat rack, the whole house shook with a thunk, as if something large had been thrown against it. He then heard a huge primal roar, and his whole body relaxed. Christine held him and he looked at her. There was no fear in her eyes, just astonishment and anger. They stood together. Sam grabbed his gun belt and cautiously walked out the front door.

"You had a visitor," Nathan said as Sam followed his pointing finger to the man, clearly dead, impaled on the side of Sam's house.

"I see you greeted him for me," Sam said as he walked over to the man on the wall.

"Kind of quiet, this guy," Sam went on.

"I only had a second. I didn't see you at the swimming hole, so I thought I'd come by to see if everything was alright." Nathan smiled a huge grin at both of them.

Christine, walked over to Nathan, reached up, and laid a hand on his shoulder, "thank you".

Nathan laid his huge paw on her shoulder and nodded that was all he had to say.

"Anyone else in the area?" Sam said.

"Not that I saw. I didn't see a car, so I was surprised to see him on your porch. And he was looking in your window, and being sneaky about it, and then I saw the gun. I didn't have time to invite him to put down his weapon. Besides, he didn't look like he came over for a social visit"

"You did what you had to, and I'm glad you did. These guys don't stop trying. That worries me. What's next? Each time they've tried a sneak attack. I'd rather a more direct confrontation, but I'm not running the show just yet. I'll drive Christine's car back home. We need to get this guy out of sight. We'll try to ID him later. Thanks again, Nathan."

"Just as long as you catch up on the lifesaving if I need it in the future."

"As a rule. Do you think you could pull the guy off the side of my house?"

"Don't you want to leave him there as a warning to your enemies?"

"I can see the headline now: Man pinned to side of Sheriff's home, seeks asylum." Besides, from the look of it, Mr. Killer and I could both hang from your spear and it still wouldn't come down."

"He might just start to ripen, Sam. We could always eat him."

"Take it easy, Nathan. Christine may not speak much English, and she's holding up better than I would if I was looking at a guy pinned to the side of her home in France. Looking at you pointing at the guy and saying "eat" can't be good."

Nathan nodded, knowing that he had a lot of stock with Sam. He had seen a subtle change in Sam and knew it was due to his relationship with Christine. Even in this time of danger, he saw that Sam had found some peace with Christine. It gave him a sense of hope and deepened his feelings for the man he considered more than a brother.

"Sorry, just blowing off steam. Is it time to get everyone together?"

"As fast as we can. I'm betting this guy is solo. When he doesn't report back, he'll be missed."

Sam steered Christine towards her vehicle, the old farm truck Madeleine used for hauling vegetables to the restaurant and jumped into the driver's seat. Christine slid over in the seat next to him. When he wasn't shifting gears, he held her hand. He felt real fear, not for himself but for her. He felt just awful. He took a chance and pulled over to the side of the road.

"I love you Christine," Sam said as he looked her in the eye.

That didn't require any translation. She looked straight back and said, "I love you Sam."

Their world had just changed, and they had just taken the first step down a new road. Something had been settled. They both relaxed a little, and Sam felt a little better.

Sam fished in his pocket for his cell phone and speed dialed his father.

"Dad, we've been attacked. Advance assassin killed, meeting at Chez-Toche."

"Understood, any wounded?"

"None."

"I am on my way"

Just hearing his father's commanding voice say those things gave Sam courage.

"Bring it on you scumbags, let's dance," he muttered under his breath, as he turned towards town.

As soon as John Trunce got the message he pushed a send button on his phone and a message was instantly sent out. He walked into the house and found Karen in the kitchen.

"Karen, get your Winchester. We need to go," John said.

She didn't say a word; she could ask questions in the jeep. She reached over the top of the kitchen door and took down a well maintained Winchester, Model 1870 lever action, cocked it, settled down the hammer, and followed John out of the room. He was all business, and on the rare occasions when she'd seen him in this mode, he was a sight to behold.

She couldn't help but ask, "Sam okay?"

"He called," he said, as he reached over and pulled her to him as they walked side by side. She exhaled forcefully in response and relaxed a little. They jumped into John's jeep and drove away from the main road, along the trail that was their shortcut to town.

"Sam knows what he's doing, and Nathan's been watching the house. Didn't tell Sam, but he's been camping out under the trees, just into the woods along the side of the house. Sounds like someone ran into Nathan or Sam under the wrong circumstances." John knew better than to use words like assassin or killer. While Karen was strong, that would be too much, too soon.

As they drove, their minds wandered back to a time when Sam was only twelve years old, scrawny, all bones and a carefree attitude. He had met Nathan while simultaneously saving his life. Promptly upon his arrival to the USA, Nathan had wandered away from his father's farm, taken a trail that led up a steep ridge and gotten too close to the edge, causing the ground under his feet to crumble and slide over the edge of a good one hundred foot drop down to rocks. He'd managed to grab onto some roots, and was dangling and started to yell. Sam was out in the woods as usual, and heard yelling in a strange language, obviously someone in trouble. He'd run like only a southern wood-rat kid can and found Nathan. Sam laid over the edge and said "Don't move," motioning with his hands. Sam could see that the roots the man was holding onto weren't going to last long. He pulled out his old Barlow knife that had been his grandfather's and cut a vine off and tried to position it over the man so he could grab on. Even the slightest movement from the man to try to get the vine and the roots slipped more. Sam could see the man was duly frightened, but he wasn't blubbering or shouting anymore. Sam didn't hesitate a second, he went down the vine to the man. The closer he got he could see it was a kid, not a man. Sam got alongside and wrapped his legs around the kid's waist and held on. Nathan then reached out for the vine, the roots broke, and for a long second, Sam remembered it as days when the two joked about it, Sam held his own weight and Nathan's then 250 pounds. They then both climbed up the vine and scrambled to the top. Just as soon as both were over and safe, the vine crashed down out of the tree that it had been attached to and slid over the side of the cliff. They were both stunned for a second, and then started to laugh uncontrollably, slapping each other on the back and mimicking the sound of the vine and pretending to have vines slip through their fingers while yelling like they were falling.

They had spent the rest of the day crashing around in the woods and made their first trip to the swimming hole after a quick stop for Nathan to check in. Neither said anything about what happened. Months later, Nathan had mentioned it to his mother when they went for a walk, learning what grew wild in their new land. She had mentioned it almost casually to a shocked Joseph, who felt duty bound to tell John. They decided that it was done, and was Sam and Nathan's business. After that they were inseparable, and spent their teen and young adult years together, until Sam ended up in college and the military and Nathan went to college for botany. Sam was home now and not going anywhere. With Sam there, Nathan was home too.

CHAPTER
TWENTY-
SEVEN

am sat in the dining room at Chez-Toche and looked around at the
people sitting at various tables all turned towards one another. They
were all men and women who had each played a pivotal role in driving
out the drug dealers when Sam returned from Detroit. TJ, Moon, Crockett,
Madeleine, Christine, John, Karen, Nathan, Joseph, Ua and John's friend
Cecil Tripoli, a retired pilot, turned to look at John as he spoke.

"There's been another attempt on Sam's, life and I have every reason to
believe the killer would have taken out Christine as well, simply for being
in the wrong place wrong time... " Just as John was about to continue,
Tracy walked in from the kitchen.

"Mon Dieu," Madeleine exclaimed. "You come and go like the north
wind."

Tracy greeted everyone around the table and sat down, "Please continue, I'll tell you what I know when you're done."

John continued and laid out each person's assignment and fall back
positions. Sam thought the plan seemed simple. It was designed so each

person knew where they were supposed to be when the fighting started and their assignments.

"Anything or anyone out of the ordinary has to be reported. Anyone of you can send the code. I would rather be safe than sorry. You are all prudent, reasonable people, some with extensive training and others with less. That doesn't matter; it's only a mistake not to notify. If you're wrong, we'll call it a dry run, no harm done. If it isn't, I think the shit will hit the fan fast. Tracy, what do you have?" John said.

"My sources tell me that the man Nathan ventilated is probably an individual known as Smith, a highly trained, first-rate hit man. He's for hire, but not for little stuff. He won't take out a spouse for you or do a simple witness-type matter. He is generally political. How he got here is not yet known, but it makes me nervous." Nobody asked how Tracy could have identified the man so quickly; they just took it for granted that Tracy had been close by.

"What about our Mexican dog walker Junior eyeballed," John pressed.

"He's a local representative of one Manny the Farmer, Mexican mob. Manny's a real businessman type. His men never talk and are rarely caught in the act of anything. He kills when necessary and plans down to the minute detail. He has connections to Cuba and the Cuban military. The DEA can't get him, he basically might as well be the authorities in Mexico, and he never sets foot in any country with an extradition treaty with the US, which doesn't matter, because we don't have anything on him anyway."

"The dog walker, who is he?" Sam asked.

"Best we can tell, Manny's nephew. He couldn't find his ass in a hall of mirrors and loses more money than he makes, but he's loyal to Manny. Manny has that aura, that skill; people do his bidding because they love him, not because they fear him. It is impossible to get into his inner sanctum. DEA lost a couple back in the 80's trying to get in. Manny probably doesn't even know about it. He is an idealist, a rags-to- riches story and he's not a thug. I think this is a personal war against the United States, and he sees poisoning the people as a means to an end, paving the way for the immigration of workers who will do the jobs that the people of the United States will no longer do, at a pay scale that they will not accept. He doesn't see migrant fruit picking as the future of the hardworking Mexican immigrant as fair or safe. He wants health care for his people, pensions, security, housing, and education. He is winning his war. Soon, American business will be completely dependent on Hispanic workers. The Meth epidemic makes it more likely to happen sooner. I'm not taking a position on it either way, other than the Meth problem is horrible and an absolute crisis. Secondly, we as a nation need to decide what we want to do or not do about the influx of workers from Mexico and all points South. We can embrace it and have a plan for the future, or we can fight it, but we can't pretend it isn't happening. I believe it's not immigration from Mexico that is the problem, it's the fact that 80% of the Meth available in this country comes from Mexico."

Nathan spoke up, "How does that translate into what we can expect?"

"It will be a military attack," Madeleine said from her table at the back of the room.

Everyone turned to Madeleine as she spoke, having broken her silence. "It will now be about honor for this Manny the Farmer, an eye for an eye. He comes, as it sounds, from humble beginnings. It seems that few men born to wealth ever have the kind of social conscience that is obvious here. People born to wealth and privilege may commiserate with 'ordinary people,' and genuinely try to help as they see fit, but they do not understand the people, their lives, concerns, or politics for that matter. The connection to Castro, another man from the rank and file, although far from ordinary, is much the same as this Manny the Farmer. I will venture a guess that they are friends." As she said this she looked meaningfully at Tracy. He spoke no words, but gave her a slow nod of agreement.

"Tell us about Cuban soldiers, Colonel," Sam said, voicing without saying what everyone was thinking.

"The ones we ran into were vicious," John said as he glanced at the men who had fought with him in Vietnam. "There was a program called the Cuban Project, torturers. Joseph and I ran across the bastards, although that wasn't our primary goal. We couldn't take action then, but these guys slowly murdered many a good man fighting for his country. I got a good look at a couple and them at me. Joseph and I lost every one else on that recon mission. They do not want to run into Colonel Trunce or Major Harper, either in this life or the next."

Joseph nodded, "No politics involved now. I see them, they die."

"For we are Masai," Ua said.

"We are Masai, princess," Joseph answered.

The meeting broke up, and each participant knew that there wouldn't be any others until there was a conclusion to the matter.

As everyone dispersed and Tracy rose to leave, Madeleine put her hand on his wrist and he hung back. Sam and the others moved out the front door and went about their business.

"Have you given any thought as to cutting off the snake's head, Filleul?" Tracy was Madeleine's godson. Madeleine and Tracy shared a kinship born of trust. Some people are capable of action without compunction or hesitation. In combat commanders identify these people as killers. Madeleine identified Tracy as such and insisted that she complete the training the espionage services of the United States had subjected Tracy to.

From the beginning, Tracy knew gender was irrelevant; he'd trained and fought alongside women in the Mossad, the respected and feared Israeli secret police. Madeleine and his family had rescued him after his capture and near death in Israel, when the PLO murdered his girlfriend and took him hostage. Seeing Madeleine in action had given him his first look at a hardened killer. He came to understand why Madeleine Toche was a legend in the small dark world of professional death.

"He's in the wind, or I would have done it myself," Tracy said.

"I sense that regardless of how this turns out, Manny the Farmer had better either stay in the wind, or retire and concede this war from his end," Madeleine said.

"Once he knows the score, I believe he will."

"I hope so for his sake," Madeleine said.

Crockett ambled out of the meeting at the restaurant looking as little like a deadly sniper as you can, fat and dumpy. He had promised himself while sick and starving in a bamboo cage as a captive of the North Vietnamese, that if he ever got home, he would never be hungry again. The thing that saved him, and helped him in his line of work as a car salesman, was his gift of gab. The Viet Cong didn't know he was a sniper, and just thought he was a jar head grunt doing what he was told.

If they'd have known all the officers and officials he'd killed, he never would have gotten a chance to get fat. He was another of John Trunce's saves. For a few years after the war he'd been a puddle. John was there to pick him up more than once, and had helped him to deal with his demons. On his way out the door, John placed a hand on his ample shoulder.

"Crockett, you are our sleeper. Just stand by and wait for contact from me in case we get into a fix."

"My rifle and I will be on alert. Okay if I stay at the car lot, Colonel?"

"Best place for you, Crockett"

John watched Crockett amble away, amazed that anyone could maintain sanity after having been starved in a cage for so long. Crockett still had his share of problems, but overall worked through them and made a life. Now, after all of that, nothing was that daunting, nothing was that stressful, after wondering day in and day out whether he would live through the day. Crockett remembered the miracle day that he was released, sick beyond measure, mostly because there were peace talks on and the North Vietnamese didn't want him, a P.O.W, to die on their hands. That was madness, this was gravy.

John walked into the spotless old hanger, where Cecil had the wing cartridge magazines open, loading a belt of large caliber bullets.

"I installed the missiles and we've got plenty of ammo for the guns. Think we'll need them?" Cecil said looking over his shoulder as John walked up.

"Depends what they come at us with and how. I want to send these guys packing. I'm not the one looking for revenge here. You've got to know that a surface to air could take you out," John said.

"He better have damn good aim when I come in. I see any kind of hand held rocket launcher and they get everything all at once," Cecil said.

"Just so you know, Moon upgraded the punch on those rockets," John said.

"How much?"

"Just don't be too close when you fire them," John said grinning.

"Singe my ass a little?"

"More like Hindenburg time. You know Moon, he likes his ordinance and he's definitely one of those 'bigger is better' guys."

"Understood. If I have to fire rockets on anyone, I might as well blast the hell out of them." Cecil said.

CHAPTER
TWENTY-
EIGHT

Paco sat comfortably in the shade of Manny's veranda sipping a little of the wonderful Agave Tequila his Patron had pressed into his hand.

"We will be ready to leave tonight, Patron. We'll move at night in the desert and make the connection on the other side two days later."

"Transportation has been arranged," Paco said. "Each man has currency and a safe location if you have to go to ground. Use your best judgment. This Sam Trunce has now not only killed several of my men, but stands as an embarrassment that a man in my position can ill afford at this stage. Tell no one else, but when you leave, I do too. I go to Cuba. When the mission is complete, come to Cuba and find me in Havana. There is a cigar maker there in the main square next to a cantina where you can leave me a message. I have purchased a modest home for you, and you will have income for life, on one condition."

"Anything Patron."

"You teach me to fish in the ocean," he said wistfully.

Paco left his employer with a new sense of resolve. This would be his last mission, the one he knew he'd have. It never was your last mission until you knew for certain that it was. It had been a long time and he was heading into the complete unknown. The intelligence seemed complete, but as an old soldier, he knew intelligence was only valuable when it was confirmed on the ground. He sensed that he had better be cautious. Smith had failed, and that was a bad sign. People can blunder into one victory, but taking out a highly trained killer was something else altogether. There was no press on it at all: he had vanished, presumably dead. They knew that the sheriff had a military background, Special Forces no less, and was a decorated Detroit detective, but he was only one man. His family and friends were around, but they were locals, older mostly, and certainly no threat to the trained men in his unit. He felt like the intelligence missed something crucial. The man had to have support, but where was it coming from? Maybe one of the deputies accidentally stumbled on the Man killed him, and the report was buried like the destruction of the van. He didn't like maybes and not knowing. They would be cautious.

Twenty men and Paco's subordinates Manolo and Philippe were seated in several plain SUV's that took them and their equipment to their crossing point, one rarely used by illegals going to the United States. The crossing here was harsh and long, and had no water. His men had been trained in the hot desert sun and had become accustomed to operating with less water as part of their preparation. They would travel light.

After leaving their SUVs, Paco and his troops made silent progress through the dessert night. It wasn't a slow amble: they moved at an easy loping pace that the Apache had called a dog trot. The men carried some gear. They would get the rest when they reached their staging area.

They had gone about ten miles into the crossing when their point man stopped abruptly and held up his hand to stop. There were voices in the distance. Paco and Manolo advanced closer, silently under cover of the scrub and sparse vegetation. Three men with weapons held a small group of men together at gunpoint. It was clear that those held were pleading for their lives. "Coyotes," Paco whispered to Manolo. These were the unpredictable and often murderous men who moved illegals across the border. Some immigrants made it, others were robbed and killed. Paco reached for his side arm, as did Manolo. They attached silencers to the pistols, stood, and shot the armed men. They then walked up and spoke to the men who had been spared.

"Thank you Patron, thank you," was about all they could manage. Paco whistled, and the remainder of his men came forward. They shared their canteens and a supply of water was given to the men. One of Paco's soldiers produced a map and gave it to one of the men.

"You follow the indications on the map, do not stray. We are on a mission and cannot help you cross. You must send word back about these Coyotes. People must not trust them. You have been spared, and I expect you to earn honest livings in the United States."

The men shook their heads in unison, shocked that they were alive, much less being helped by men who seemed to drop out of the clear night sky.

Paco gathered the men and they were gone as quickly as they had arrived. As he jogged, Paco thought of his own Patron and his various businesses. Paco thought that some of them were less than honorable, but Manny was no Coyote and his activities had a purpose. Over all, Paco agreed, the United States wouldn't control the Americas forever, especially as the Hispanic population grew. Those governments and the people who ran them that embraced that change and what it meant for this part of the world would prepare the peoples of South, Central and North America for worldwide competition in the immediate future. Europe had already established itself as a trading block and China was fast on it's heels doing the same. The rest of the world seemed to be up for grabs, and it was a game of who would get there first as the resources, natural and otherwise, would be controlled. One day Americans wouldn't only be identified by the region or country they came from, but from the super continent that would be comprised of all of the Americas. Survival demanded it. Not only for the smaller, developing countries but for the United States as well. He felt a little older, and found contemplating geopolitical issues tiring. The real work in those areas would come from the men and women of the coming generations. He was an old soldier. His crusade was coming to an end.

One day later, Paco and his men met a large Winnebago motor home a good ten miles on the US side of the border. Paco greeted Carlos as the men boarded the vehicle and took seats throughout. Paco sat in the comfortable front passenger seat, grateful for the cushions after a night spent on his feet.

The rest of the vehicle had been altered to accommodate more bunks. The weapons were stowed in a compartment in the floor of the vehicle, and the men stretched out comfortably in the bunks after their grueling crossing. There was plenty of water and beer to give the men a reward, but also to replenish some carbohydrates. Two of the men busied themselves in the kitchenette, and the chatter was light hearted.

"Well, Carlos, what do you think of the mission?" Paco said.

"I would leave this one alone, but I do not make the decisions," he said with a meaningful glance to Paco.

"Luckily, neither does Manny's nephew, who you and I know to be an imbecile," Paco said.

"I'm glad you said it. No disrespect to the Patron, but if the Patron retires as he has said he will, so will I. I don't need much, and have some money put away in cash deposits here and in the Caribbean. I could easily go fishing for the rest of my life, read, take long siestas and ponder the mysteries of the universe and how they are revealed in a Brazilian cut bikini," Carlos said.

"We certainly think alike my friend, and I think you will be on the beach before you know it. Now I need a rest. Give us a little break and then one of us will drive. If we get pulled over you just hop back into the seat, the other brothers and I will sleep," Paco said.

"Brothers?" Carlos asked.

"That's our cover, we're Monks."

"Sleep well, Abbot," Carlos said.

"I will pray for you, my son."

Twenty hours later, the Winnebago pulled into a pole barn. Manolo jumped out and closed the door behind him. The men exited the trailer and assembled in a line next to it. Jose strode up, looking like a cross between a pimp and Patton. Paco and the others looked at him, hoping it was some kind of a joke to put the men at ease. He began to inspect the men. Paco let him do so, and to their credit, the men acted the part.

"Good, good. These men are ready, Paco."

"They are ready," he intentionally omitted any reference to Jose's position of authority.

"Paco, a word," Jose said, raising an eyebrow.

Jose walked over to a small room off of the staging area and Paco followed with a nod to the men.

Once in the room Jose began to speak, in a tight voice, "I am in charge..."

He didn't have time to finish, as Paco closed the door, backed him into a wall, and simultaneously grabbed his testicles.

"I see that I have your attention. I am in command, read this." He held a note in Manny's handwriting under Jose's nose.

"Dear Nephew, Paco is in charge, do everything that he tells you to do. If you don't, I am sure that he will kill you. Good luck, Uncle Manny." Jose read the note disbelievingly.

Once Jose had read the note, Paco released him, "We understand one another, Jose. You will do as I say. If you do not, and one of my men gets killed, I will feed you piece by piece to your own dog. By the way, what is his name?"

"Lion," Jose said, clearly whipped.

"Well, there you go then."

CHAPTER
TWENTY-
NINE

Tucked away on a remote farm property thirty miles west of Patience, Paco, Manolo, Philippe, and Carlos sat down around a picnic table inside the pole barn where the men were relaxing and examined a map. Landmarks around the town of patience were highlighted along with Sam's home. Other areas were marked, including his parent's home, Madeleine's restaurant, and the homes of several Deputies. The map had been carefully prepared showing various ingress and egress points.

"We need to do this as quickly as possible, targeting those people who are connected to the Sheriff. I believe that we will have to use those individuals to get to him. Surprise didn't work the last time, and few people are as good as the Man. We will assume that we cannot take him by surprise. We must kill him and any collaterals and carry out our mission. We kill the sheriff and his immediate family and any other law enforcement officers who get in the way. Then we head to the extraction point and disappear," Paco said gesturing to various points designated on the map.

"We will have to use some of Jose's men to fill out our ranks," Manolo said.

"Carlos, are there any among those men who have some experience?" Philippe asked.

"We could get half a dozen out of that group, a few have military experience."

"I think that we're going to need to hold that restaurant. We'll move in on Sunday. They're closed midday for a big family meal, very French. Chances are the Sheriff might be headed that way anyway, he seems pretty tight with those people," Philippe added.

"Is there any chance of resistance there?" Paco said.

"Only an old woman, her granddaughter and a boy, aged twelve to thirteen."

"No men?" Paco asked.

"No, but the whole town goes there to eat. If we're not going to attract attention, then we have to strike early in the morning."

"The mission there will be to hold the women and the boy and wait for the Sheriff to arrive, or in the alternative to get him to trade himself for them. We'll then take him and eliminate him. No theatrics, we'll do it cleanly. He will simply disappear. We'll send a few men to his parent's farm, to find the additional targets," Paco said.

"We can avoid anyone seeing us. Jose's men are thugs anyway, and can disappear into one of Manny's other areas for a while," Manolo said.

"We all look the same to them anyway," Carlos laughed, and the others joined in.

For the rest of the day, the men were divided into three squads of six men each. Paco headed up one of them, Manolo and Philippe the other two. Carlos selected four men who would go to the restaurant, where no action was anticipated. Carlos brought the men forward and Paco sat them down.

"Simple mission: hold an old woman, her granddaughter, and great grandson hostage, so that we can grab the sheriff and if possible avoid unnecessary bloodshed. There will be no harm done to the people at the restaurant. Do not give them a reason to remember your faces." Paco appraised the men as he addressed them. They all had the rough-around-the-edges look of men on their side of the law. Nothing jumped out at him; they each met his eye for the most part and said nothing.

"You will drive up in a delivery van and gain access to the building through the rear door. Separate them and keep in contact at no more than ten minute intervals. You will be issued weapons and secure communication equipment. Any deviation will be severely dealt with."

All three men nodded, stood and made their way back towards the tables where the other men sat waiting for the midday meal.

Jose watched from the other side of the pole barn, seething internally. He hated Paco and everything military, his own brief stint in the Mexican military having been anything but memorable. Apparently his sergeant had not been impressed with his connections, having had some of his own. Jose could still feel the toe of his boot in his ass. He should have been given better instruction with that rocket launcher before being ordered to fire it. He grimaced a little at the memory of the noncom Officers' latrine detonating and being ordered to dig the new one by hand. He was not meant for such indignity, and this Paco was the absolute embodiment of every maniacal drill sergeant or officer he'd ever encountered. Now Jose was in charge. These were his men, and they would follow his orders.

Grab my balls? Well Mr. Paco, you might just die in combat. Accidents do happen. This was his chance to show his uncle that he could be trusted with the most important of missions, not just making drugs and selling them to the Anglos. As for that bastard Carlos, this was something that he was going to do with his own men with his own plan. He didn't trust that man. He always seemed to be second guessing him, if only with his eyes. He walked to the small farm house on the property that had been rented, sight unseen, through a local contact. Inside, his men were sitting around the living room, playing cards, watching TV, and drinking beer and tequila. He motioned to three of the toughest looking men and the ones who had been selected by Carlos, and took them into a small side room, set up with a desk, phone, and computer.

"Men, I need your utmost loyalty. We are being left out of the true objective here, which is to avenge the death of our compadres and send a message that we will do as we please without interference. It is us who will take this sheriff and remove him. My uncle's true intention is for blood to avenge blood. We will take this man and his disappearance will be a warning to all. It is I who will be the true Patron soon, and your loyalty to me will be rewarded. You will be my captains and share in the bounty."

The men looked at Jose, and nodded when they thought it was time to do so. In various stages of inebriation, just about anything their benefactor said was fine. He kept them in money, booze, and women at this point, and that was all that was important. More money, booze and women sounded good. One of the men managed, "Not a word Patron, we will do as you say and this gringo cop will pay."

"Tomorrow, when the others have left, we will arrive before them, take the sheriff, and have him when the great Carlos and Paco show up."

Jose could tell that his men didn't mix with Paco's men and clearly didn't like them. Thugs as they were, they didn't like either people as pathetic as themselves or people they couldn't push around.

The feeling was returned; the looks that some of them got were definitely meaningful. Soldier boys, thought they were tough. Well, maybe they were, but enforcement through violence, now that was their line of work.

"Now go and have some drinks, but turn in early. We will be on the most important job of our lives in the morning."

He clapped them all on their backs as they walked out of the room, sat down at the desk and looked over the map and diagram of the sheriff's house that Paco had distributed. He reached down and scratched Lion's ear as the dog lay on his side, whimpering and pumping his legs, asleep halfway through some dream race. Even in his sleep he keeps himself in training, he thought. I too have trained my whole life for this day. My future is made. I will have the Hacienda and the high-born wife, and I will leave this country for good. People will send me money, and I will be the law.

"There should be no problems tomorrow. Jose will stay here. We will bring the sheriff here and eliminate him. We will make his bones disappear with the body with chemicals that we have at hand. Then, we will return to the Winnebago and drive back to the border and into Mexico, a job well done." Paco breathed a sigh of relief.

"What if we encounter resistance?" Manolo questioned.

"We will kill all combatants, anyone who takes up arms against us. There will be no prisoners."

The men nodded, and remembered their long ride from the border and knew that if they were caught, they would never see their wives and girlfriends again.

CHAPTER
THIRTY

Sam woke early and trudged out of bed and down the stairs to make coffee. He simply did not care whether coffee was good or bad for you. There was enough misery in life without denying yourself everything.

As soon as there was a trickle in the pot, Sam put another cup under the stream of coffee and poured himself the first run, ironically a bootlegging term. Must be spending too much time with Nathan, he thought. He plopped himself down on his sofa, facing the window that overlooked the meandering little offshoot of the main creek that wandered back on his property and through his family's and Nathan's land. As long as nobody polluted the stream and the land stayed in their families, it was a tie that bound them all together. As he drank his coffee his thoughts drifted to Christine, not only the physical memories, but more so what life would be like with her and her son. Some men don't want to get into a relationship with women with kids, but his knew his heart had already been captured twice over, once by Christine and once by the boy. He caught himself planning their lives and smiled. He hadn't thought much of marriage and a family, although he was now definitely past his youth. The creaks, moans, pops, and protests of his body when he got out of bed were proof of that. He had casually told his parents once that he felt old. They laughed outright at him, in that telling way people do when you say something downright stupid. John got a hold of himself first and slapped Sam on the back. "Forty ain't old boy. Hell, you haven't even reached the first water station on this marathon!"

Sam might have argued, but knew if he did he would just be talking out of his ass, so he decided to learn from the experience instead.

Sam threw on some old workout shorts and walked out to his barn, where he had a few pieces of equipment for doing pull-ups, leg presses, pushups, and the like. He did it all slowly and deliberately without pause, and was done in fifteen minutes. He certainly didn't need to get any bigger. He'd learned a long time ago that you can kill yourself in the gym, but there's always somebody bigger, unless you're Nathan. As he was catching his breath, Sam heard the distinct and unmistakable sound of his dad's dog howling in the trees behind his house. The skin on his arms and legs grew goose bumps as the realization hit him. He tore towards the house and his cell phone. As he neared the front door he caught a glimpse of two men raising shotguns and firing. He twisted and threw himself through the door and a few pellets stung into his shoulder as the right side of the door frame blew apart. He could hear the men coming fast behind him as he scrambled for the kitchen, where he knew his pistol was sitting on the table. Feet crashed onto the porch as Sam scrambled for the kitchen. He stumbled and heard a shell being racked into a shotgun, and cranked his head around to see the shotgun raised to fire directly at him. Just as he anticipated the blast, the gunman went down in a tangle of snarl and fur. Gingas was tearing into the man. Sam leapt into the kitchen and snatched his gun, running wildly back into the living room, where the second man was aiming to shoot the dog. Sam fired three times in succession, catching the man in the chest, belly, and face, throwing him backwards as the big bore magnum launched him back out the front door. Sam took a quick look out the window in time to see three more men coming his way with assault rifles.

"Time to go!" he yelled, and to his surprise the big dog followed him out the back door and towards the squad. The big dog figured it out and leapt through the driver's side window. Sam heard the machine guns open up, but they were missing their mark as he sprinted and dove through the window. Most people assume that if you're firing an automatic weapon, you'll hit everything you're shooting at, but moving targets are moving targets. Complicate that with the other guy blasting back at you with a weapon that will take your head off your shoulders, and aim is more like the old 'hit em and hope' pool shot, where you blast the cue ball into a group of balls and hope one of yours goes down.

Sam crashed into the squad. He twisted the key and threw the vehicle into drive and spun it around. Bullets plinked into the body and windshield, but were stopped by the armor T.J. had installed. The squad roared and shot towards one of the men who spun and fired on full automatic, trying to slow the vehicle down. Sam stomped on the accelerator and simply ran the man down. The man hit the radiator and disappeared beneath the car. Sam didn't slow down and felt the rear tires bounce over the body. There was a bit of a bump, but more of a crunch. Something skittered across the hood and kept going. The windmill that Sam and Nathan had spent hours rebuilding went up with a whoomp! and shards of wood went everywhere. The dog had wisely hunkered down in the back seat, obviously thinking maybe he made the wrong decision, Sam thought. He could see several men coming from the woods now with automatic weapons. It wasn't a rag-tag rush either. These men came in a skirmish line. Not good. Sam spun the wheel and the spinning tires found traction on his gravel road. He was fishtailing and sliding all over the place as he shot down his driveway and onto the main road.

As his tires got traction on the pavement the positraction kicked in, Sam smelled the stink of burning rubber as the tires roasted. But for the weight of the vehicle he would simply have slid off the road as the front end came up. The vehicle wanted to do those things, but was just a hair too heavy and instead launched down the road like a shot out of a cannon. There was smoke everywhere and the shooting had stopped momentarily. Sam punched the send button on the cell phone mounted to his dash and sent the signal out to his friends preprogrammed numbers. He flew past the restaurant and down towards his parents' road. He thought about trying to call to warn his dad, but he would have heard some of the commotion. A rocket had blown up his windmill. Sam was extra pissed because the windmill worked and actually put some juice back into the grid and the batteries in his barn, funny, the practical things that were going through his mind while he was taking automatic gunfire. The dog was now in the front seat, sitting calmly, looking out the passenger side window. Up close, he was huge, Sam thought. At least 200 pounds and all muscle, teeth, and mean. People tend to equate size in wild animals with corresponding size in a human being. Wrong. Sam thought about the damage a chimp can do to a person, or a cute little badger or wolverine, for that matter. A 200 pound dog that is half wolf is a bad thing, even to a 1200 pound Grizzly Bear, much less a man.

John heard Gingas first, and immediately hit the send button on his own cell. Karen was at Madeleine's, and he had to trust that she was safe. Seconds later he heard the first crash of gunfire. It sounded like a shotgun. He ran to his barn and fired up his jeep.

"Come on boy, come on boy," he tensely muttered waiting to hear return fire and then he did, the big crash of a three shot pattern.

"That's Special Forces shooting back, you bastards!" he screamed. "Shooting god damn back!"

More gunfire and the unmistakable sound of that crazy squad firing up. He thought of all the jokes Sam had endured about that noisy, ridiculous machine. He thanked God for it now. Then he heard the detonation of the rocket, but the squad roared on. The fight was coming. He drove the jeep to the edge of the trail leading into the woods and waited. It would be a matter of seconds. Just as he jumped out of the driver's seat for a second, he heard a single shot and an instant burning sensation as a bullet grazed his upper back. He threw himself to the ground and heard another single, far off shot, but nothing hit near him. Jerry's in the trees, he thought. Old habits die hard. No matter how many battles he'd fought it was the endless slog, from D-day to Germany and the end of the War that he lived every day. His combat in Korea and Vietnam had been every bit as terrifying but, as an officer, more controlled. He could have avoided almost all of it, but he could not sit still while his men were in danger. He just couldn't.

Sam came careening around the corner and slammed the squad sideways at the end of the bridge that crossed the creek onto his father's property. Sam threw open the door and, as he sprinted away, he glimpsed the big dog disappear into the woods. He saw his dad crouched down by the jeep and the red stain across his back. He yelled, "Dad!"

"Sniper, just creased me, I think somebody got him."

"Crockett's out there. If he saw a muzzle flash, that dude is done," Sam said.

Sam and John leapt into the jeep and John accelerated into the trees and up the trail.

"I think we've engaged the enemy, boy!" John said, bouncing around in the seat. Sam held on as best he could. Army jeeps of that vintage were only marginally comfortable for the driver, who had something to hold onto. Passengers were often tossed and the vehicles rolled. John had added a roll bar and welded on a couple of grab bars. He didn't want to jettison any passengers on just such an occasion as this.

"Joseph and Nathan?"

"Joseph will be in the trench by now. Nathan is roaming, according to plan. Trench warfare was not made for giants. Nathan moves best at top speed, crashing across the African plains or through the Missouri woods. Besides, apparently the farther away from you, the better," he grinned.

"I suppose that holds true for everybody," Sam said flatly.

"Just remember there Hondo, this isn't only about you. I was born in this county and a lot of people see this as an attack on their way of life, their little corner of peace and solitude in the world. These bastards think they can come in here and poison our children and then punish us when we retaliate. When every single one of us is dead, then they can try."

Sam realized he was getting a little bit of a civics lesson from a man who had defended his country and way of life abroad and saw this as an attack directly on his home. You didn't stand around and wait for somebody in authority to tell you it was ok to defend yourself, you just did it.

"Once we blast these clowns to hell, we'll give Tracy a call," he offered. John flashed him a grin and a firm nod, and yelled, "Airborne!"

Jose watched in shocked disbelief as the huge animal tore past him and leapt onto the back of his man. The Uzi he held in his hand dropped to his side, and his mouth dropped open in disbelief. Lion crouched down on the ground behind him making his body as small as possible. What the hell was that? A damn werewolf for Christ's sake? He ran towards the house just as the man broke cover and dove into his squad. He yelled "fire," and the backup man fired the rocket at the vehicle, game over, he thought. Then, suddenly everything went wrong. The rocket skipped across the hood of the car and blew up the windmill. He screamed into his walkie-talkie that was connected to his men at the restaurant, but got nothing but static.

CHAPTER
THIRTY-ONE

Madeleine, Christine, Yves and Karen worked in the kitchen and were half listening and half watching a French football match on the television. When Karen called it soccer they all corrected her in unison. They were all in a good mood, as the Sunday meal was always a highlight of the week: great food, lazy and unhurried, real living, nowhere to rush off to.

Madeleine had gone down to the cellar to bring up some new wine that she had just gotten in. A little kitchen prep tippling was in order. It was just then that a delivery van pulled up to the back door.

Christine looked out and saw some company name on the side and thought it must be a delivery, but on Sunday? Just as she walked to the door, three men burst in. Christine tried to push back but was overpowered and thrown backwards into the heavy center chopping station, striking her head as she fell. Yves ran at the man who had hurt his mother. He was struck forcefully by the stock of a rifle and fell back, knocking down his chair and falling into the wall. Karen had no time to react and had a gun pushed into her face.

Madeleine heard the commotion upstairs and the cries of Christine and Yves and the yelling of the men. It took everything she had not to charge up the stairs. She had no weapon downstairs, and silently cursed herself for moving unarmed. Besides, she reminded herself, even if she had a bunch of guns going off in a confined space, the chances were everyone was going to get shot. It wasn't like the movies. She'd seen dead men fire weapons their fingers locked on the trigger. She needed something, though. She glanced quickly around the room and knew she only had seconds. A head count would show that she was gone and undoubtedly a door leading off the kitchen would get opened first. Damn it! So much clutter down here. Her mind raced and then she saw it: on a shelf was an old kit bag. The one her husband had carried throughout the war and used on fishing trips. She hurried over to it and ripped it open. A small wash kit was inside with an old fashioned straight razor. She grabbed it and put it down the front of her pants. It wasn't the first time in her life she'd hidden something there. She knew the value of that hiding place depended on the nature and experience of the man or woman searching you. Some just didn't search you down there. Most idiots, or the untrained, look in more places when they buy a car than when searching a prisoner. She just had time to turn around and grab a bottle of wine when the door burst open.

"Don't move," a burly looking man with a wicked scar along the right side of his face yelled.

Madeleine purposefully dropped the bottle and began a weepy pleading cry, "Don't hurt me, don't hurt me."

The man came over and roughly grabbed her by the arm and pushed her ahead of him up the steps. She stumbled into the kitchen and caught herself on a shelf of pots and pans. Christine cried out and tried to get up and was roughly grabbed by the hair and thrown back down to the floor. Madeleine saw that Yves was bleeding profusely and went over to him. The men allowed her to do so and she cradled his head in her hands and lap. She could tell that the wound was minor, and like most head wounds, was bleeding freely. She also knew that the bleeding would lessen and clot up soon. This was maybe a few stitch cut.

"Now that we have your attention, there will be nothing but absolute obedience," the larger scarred man said.

"Search them," he commanded.

"I will search this one," a ratty looking man said, and motioned for Christine to stand up. The other men leered and watched as Ratty pushed Christine up against a wall and slowly ran his hands over the entire length of her body, paying special attention to her breasts and crotch area, he whispered to her and then said aloud, "This your Mommy, brat? I like her. She's going to take care of me later." Christine bit back a yell, terrified for her grandmother and her son.

"Follow the plan and separate them. The old women stay here. The boy goes in the basement, this one upstairs," the leader instructed.

"Do as they say, Christine," Madeleine wailed like a lost, terrified child. Christine heard her say the words, but when she met her eye she saw something there she had never seen before. She'd seen her grandmother angry, agitated, happy, but what she saw now was animal, blank and bottomless. Even under these circumstances she shivered involuntarily and allowed herself to be dragged away.

Madeleine sat down on a bench with Karen beside her as the two men who were left in the room pointed their guns at them. She thought that to her credit, Karen was holding up well, this not being a natural occurrence for her. Karen had been patted down with no enthusiasm or effort. They hadn't even bothered with her, an old, terrified biddy. She would play this role the same way she had played the amorous, foolish French sex-pot all those years ago. She'd killed so many that way she could not see their faces. She remembered a few and guessed that maybe those were the ones that tugged at her conscience a little, until she thought of her brother and her comrades in the resistance and ordinary townsfolk shot based on information from a collaborator. A few had been her friends who made a bad choice and threw in with the wrong side. She killed them too, and made sure they saw who did it, as punishment for their crimes against their friends, families, and France.

Karen sat, touching Madeleine, and the two held hands like frightened children. Karen could feel Madeleine's relaxed posture and the cool dryness of her hands. She instantly knew it wasn't the gunmen who were in control. Her thoughts shifted to John and Sam and the others, and realized that these men who came to do them harm were quite literally up against the best. As her mind worked she saw each person for whom they were, and felt her own resolve strengthen.

"Do you want something to eat? We were making a meal?" Madeleine said to the leader, her head bowed and submissive.

The leader looked at the other man who shrugged and said, "Can't hurt."

The first man then motioned to Madeleine and Karen, with the short, wicked looking gun hanging down from a strap over his shoulder. The women stood up and resumed working on the vegetables and the meat that were on the counter.

"I see a knife move and I don't like it, I shoot, got it?" The leader said.

"Oh yes, of course," Karen said picking up the demure tone Madeleine was using. Good girl, Madeleine thought, she's on board. Just don't get in my way, she thought.

Ratty followed Christine up the stairs watching every sway and contour of her body. The rape he was planning excited him even more than her beauty. He pushed her in his hurry up the stairs and into the main bedroom. He threw her onto the bed face down and told her to take off her clothes. Christine glared at him, ready to kill.

"You will be very nice to me, very nice, or I will personally carve up that little boy down there right in front of you."

"No," Christine hadn't gotten all the words but knew that for Yves's sake she would have to go along, buy time, anything. This wasn't over for her. Instead of fear she felt an all-consuming anger. Patience, she heard her grandmother's voice in her mind say, patience.

As one of the men sat at a small table in the kitchen with his weapon in front of him, he drank from an open bottle of brandy he'd found on a shelf. The other man watched the two women more or less intently, and now and then walked over for a swig from the bottle. Madeleine knew there was little time, and the worst was probably starting to happen upstairs. She couldn't let that cloud her mind just yet. Christine was strong. It flamed her hate as the thought crossed her mind. Hate was the difference between the living and the dead, at least it had always been that way in her world. That was her secret. She could act without hesitation, completely without humanity. And then she did.

Just as the first man set the bottle back down and walked the few paces back to the counter, Madeleine absently knocked an onion to the floor. The man reflexively stooped to pick it up. His body was between Madeleine and the man seated at the table. She too crouched down and reached for the onion allowing the man to pick it up which he did with his trigger hand. Before he could straighten all of the way, Madeleine reached into her pants, and in one fluid move flipped open the razor, slit his throat and pushed him back into the table. This caused the seated man to be pushed back while he had the brandy bottle up for a drink. Madeleine stepped to the side of the table, and pulled a butcher knife from the block and plunged it into the base of his throat and twisted it to do the most damage, severing his jugular and slicing through his vocal cords. She pushed him to the floor, pulling out the knife, and turned back to the other man. Karen had already pushed a knife bodily through the man from behind. The whole operation had taken seconds. Without another word, Madeleine kicked off her and shoes and reached into the pantry, retrieving one of John's guns.

"I go for Christine. Leave the boy for now and watch the yard."

Madeleine moved swiftly up the stairs, making no sound in her bare feet. She wasted no time. She threw open the door and saw the ratty man starting to climb onto Christine from behind. She opened up from the hip and Christine saw his chest explode, splashing blood down onto her. She simultaneously grabbed the man and flung him sideways as she slid out. Madeleine looked at Christine and there was no fear, no revulsion, just pure animal hate. She was magnificent with her mane of wild hair about her shoulders, her naked body streaked with the blood of her enemy. It was when Christine spit on the dead man's riddled body that Madeleine knew there would always be somebody to take care of her family as long as there were women in the family like Christine.

Once downstairs, the women wrapped old blankets around the men's' bodies and dragged them into the back of the van, but not before Madeleine had taken their wallets. All of which, as she suspected, were full of cash. "Men like these do not have bank accounts. Christine, does Yves have a college fund?" Madeleine asked in French.

"Non, grand mere."

"He does now," she said, and poured a stiff drink of her best brandy for herself, Christine, and Karen. Christine let Yves out of the basement and he ran into his mother's arms. He then ran over to Madeleine and hugged her.

"Everything is okay now, mon char," she said, inspecting his head. Yves looked around wide eyed at the blood on the kitchen floor.

"Everything is fine, thanks to your great-grandmother," Karen said as she raised her glass in a toast, her own Winchester not far from her side.

Madeleine smiled and opened a drawer and pulled out a pack of Gauloises, strong French cigarettes, and fired one up.

Christine laughed, "Those are bad for you grand mere."

"Many things are bad for you," she smiled and blew out her smoke, standing there in her bare feet.

Joseph snapped the phone shut and turned to his wife. "That was John, time to go."

She was all action. Just as she was grabbing her own weapon, a cruel looking side by side shotgun, Nathan came charging into the yard.

"You got the call, Dubwana?" Joseph said, using Nathan's Masai name.

"I did, I am on my way to my area near the ridge."

The three hugged quickly and Ua put her hand on Nathan's shoulder and quickly spoke in Swahili, "Make your ancestors proud, fierce son of the Masai."

"I will kill the enemies of my people, for the glory of the Masai, my family and my friends."

With that Nathan ran out of the yard as his parents watched him go. As he picked up speed he was all midnight grace, a blur of corded muscle, shining spears. He had taken off the bright clothing of the Masai, wearing only a grey pair of shorts. The remainder of his body was painted in great swaths of grey and green paint, just as John Trunce had taught him, time and time again. He was a ghost crashing through the woods, a wraith of immense power seeking glory in battle.

"I wouldn't want to run into him out there," Joseph said.

"Nor would I, for he is your son, a great warrior," Ua said as she laid her hand on Joseph's shoulder.

Joseph and Ua looked into each other's eyes and she touched him on the cheek. Grabbing her gun and extra clips, she slipped into the seat of the produce truck, headed to the restaurant. John slung his rifle over his shoulder and drove his jeep into the woods.

CHAPTER
THIRTY-
TWO

Joseph, Sam, and John all arrived at the top of the ridge together. There was a good sized area at the end of the line to pull the vehicles into, protected from three sides. Both John and Joseph backed their vehicles in and under a canopy of heavy oak logs that had been felled and dragged into position, some time ago. John had more than one defensible position located on his property. He'd been working more on this one as of late, using his old farm tractor to do the heavy lifting.

"I'm surprised you haven't taken the time to build a concrete bunker up here, Rommel," Sam quipped.

"I believe in being able to move. Who knows what these guys have. Rockets for sure, but if I see a flame thrower, we're out." Joseph nodded in firm agreement. Sam had never seen a flamethrower used in combat but knew Joseph and his father had. Although he didn't say it, he figured it was far more likely that his father would produce a flamethrower than the enemy.

Paco stood over Jose with his boot squarely on his chest. "You fool, what did you think you would accomplish? We now have more dead and the enemy is aware of our presence."

"I should have been in charge, my uncle will hear of this," he screamed.

"What he will hear is that you died gloriously in battle if I lose one man, you worm. I don't care about your so-called men."

What Paco wasn't telling Jose was that as a precautionary measure he had distributed his men around the Trunce family compound. He had guessed correctly that the sheriff was a careful and prepared man. He once again felt vindicated in his insistence on preparation, having made sure his men were trained and experienced in the use of firepower. He fully intended to carry out his threat. Right now he didn't have time to think about it.

Paco spoke into a small radio mouthpiece that connected him to Philippe and Manolo, "Echo two, this is echo one, report."

"Echo one, this is Echo two, converging from east, cart path trail confirmed, vehicle passed through and trail leads upland to ridge area, sealing off this escape route."

"Echo one, Echo three, troops advancing along skirmish line inland North and West, confirm exit cart path mined, Claymores set."

"Determine enemy position and hold position 100 yards," Paco instructed.

As they had trained for just such a contingency, his men had set Claymore antipersonnel mines, quickly and effectively cutting off a mad dash retreat. What was now becoming evident was that the man had some stronghold position on the top of that ridge to hole up in, maybe a cave or some other kind of fortified position. His information was that the man was military and Special Forces, that was easy to get. These days a kid with some spare time on a rainy afternoon could get your life story. The man would be able to hold out for a while, but a well-placed RPG would end the story right there. Time was a consideration, although Paco didn't expect any interference from the deputies would amount to much. Any real help was more than an hour away, once someone called for help. Besides, his ace in the hole was now in a holding pattern high above Patience. His pilot, a Cuban ex-fighter jock, could land that small commercial jet on a dime or a stretch of highway, whichever was the most convenient.

CHAPTER
THIRTY-
THREE

John, Sam, and Joseph spread out through the trench, checking equipment and preparing for the pursuit they knew was coming. The front of the trench was built up slightly to provide better visibility but still dug in for protection from bullets and whatever else the enemy intended to fire at them. Two walls projected back from the front wall, making a three sided box that afforded the men a fast means of escape. The terrain behind the fortified area was heavily mined. Any attack from the rear would devastate any force coming from that direction. As Sam hurried to ready the heavy machine gun in his position, he remembered that he was wearing only shorts and no shoes. His father tossed him some boots and fatigues from a sealed plastic box, tucked into a small, hollowed-out area in the middle of the trench. John had designed the trench with fall back positions to the inner most one at the rear of the enclosure. That one was in case they couldn't get out and to the vehicles, a decision they all knew would become extremely apparent almost right away. John and Joseph scanned the woods below the ridge for activity. They both could feel the enemy out there, but they didn't come rushing up. All three men would have preferred that. Their experience told them that the enemy was cautious, and that meant preparedness and training. If these men had military training, they might be setting explosives. It wasn't a great secret of military intelligence, it was just modern warfare.

"How are we set for Claymores, Colonel?" Joseph asked.

"I used a few remote detonate pieces. I didn't want some fool kid or one of the dogs to get blown up," John said.

Sam smiled. That big monster that had saved his life was no ordinary dog. He would never think of Genghis in the same way again. That animal could think. Maybe not in a way he understood, but it had saved his ass.

"Where is Genghis dad?"

"Don't know, but he's around. He knows what guns are and what men do with them. He'll stay out of the line of fire."

"He was in the right place at the right time," Sam said.

Just then TJ called from behind a tree in a low but clear voice, "Coming in, Colonel."

All three men looked at TJ with a pronounced sense of respect. The smaller man looked just like his Mayan ancestors: small, fine featured, and the deep bronze color of the people of the equator.

"You a LRP, TJ?" Sam said.

"Mike Force," TJ said.

Sam had been a small boy when his father and Joseph were crawling around the jungles of Southeast Asia but he had heard during his own training about the Long Range Patrols, or LRPs and the specialized Special Forces Mobile Strike Force, Mike Force.

"He wore the tiger. Report," John grunted.

"I came through two lines spread out side by side. I could smell a third one, I think."

"Strength?"

"Enough. At least twenty and they're placing enough Claymores to make things damn interesting."

"What about Nathan? Dad, he could charge into a tripwire. I better go find him."

"Sam, remember I trained you and Nathan. He is a brilliant man. Smarter than you or I am and practical. I told him to stay on the periphery and to watch first. He will be up a tree to start and know where the mines are located in his area."

"You're right," Sam said, breathing a little easier.

"Colonel, the enemy is well armed. I saw at least one rocket launcher and heavy machine gun. The guys I eyeballed looked calm, ready and well trained."

"I expected a professional force. But we have the advantage. They expect a bunch of old farmers," John said as the men dispersed along the front of the trench, watching and waiting.

CHAPTER
THIRTY-
FOUR

Crockett saw the muzzle flash when his Colonel was hit. He responded. He didn't determine whether John was moving. He had his orders and one chance to respond. John had told him since there had been an assassination attempt on Sam that a sniper was all but guaranteed, and if so needed to be neutralized. Crockett did not want the sniper repositioning, so his chance was now. He sighted the fifty caliber and scanned for the sniper. The guy was in a guile suit, and almost invisible, except to another sniper. Crockett was in his own suit made to accommodate his girth. Without hesitation he adjusted for wind and elevation and put one through the man's brain. Mechanically he moved back, keeping concealed and moving into a blind that he'd constructed a couple of hundred yards away. He didn't need to radio in to John, the fifty sounded like a damn cannon, the report pealing across the valley like thunder. He'd taken a quick glimpse, relieved to see the old warrior moving with ease, must have incredible luck to have survived this long. Or God was on his side. Crockett smiled when he thought of all the armies that felt that God was on their side. Usually there were only two sides, so how the hell did that work?

Nathan lay along the length of a branch, high up in the canopy of a massive oak tree. He'd only just made it into the blind constructed up in the crotch of the old giant. He had been up this tree countless times in the past, but it had been a while. It was a little work getting up here. Maybe he needed to climb a little more often. He watched as the soldiers moved below him. Even to his untrained eyes, they looked like they knew what they were doing. He was worried, not for himself but for his friends, especially Sam. He knew John was as fierce as they come but Sam was capable of anything and would immediately put himself between harm and his friends or family. Then he came to a conclusion. We just won't let that happen, and it won't if John Trunce has anything to say about it. He waited until the men were well past and crept down the tree. He followed at a discrete distance and made sure there were no stragglers bringing up the rear. Nathan watched as the men strung wire from Claymores and noted the spots. He had spent so much time in these woods and was in them several times each week, especially in the recent past since they'd begun preparing for an attack. His father and he were botanists and had an ongoing competition about who could identify any new species. They had each discovered and named new ones themselves, to make the point that people need to explore their own environments and stop destroying them. The loss of knowledge due to the destruction of rain forest itself was incalculable. Nathan contained his natural instinct to charge on in. He knew it wouldn't be long now.

"We've got movement, Colonel," TJ said.

"Confirmed on my side," Sam said.

"Nothing yet here," Joseph said as he scanned down the slope.

"What are your orders, Colonel?" Joseph continued.

"We engage, this needs to end here and now. They want it, they brought it."

With that, John loudly cranked back the Browning fifty caliber machine gun positioned on the rim of the trench, surrounded by sand bags concealed with dirt and leaves, and opened fire. Simultaneously, the other men did so as well, aiming either towards the men they'd spotted or into likely cover positions.

Paco spaced his men carefully at the bottom of the hill leading up to the fortified position along the ridge. Although well hidden, someone had prepared that position for assault. Paco's unease grew as he realized that he had no idea the number of men that held that position. Had their attack been expected? Were they forewarned? The more he thought about it the angrier he became. That fool Jose had destroyed their advantage of surprise. Regardless, he will be a casualty. He looked at his men dispersed throughout the trees. These woods were a strange environment to a man who lived and worked in the desert. It wasn't jungle like those in Southeast Asia, but they had their forbidding denseness. He suddenly knew the advantage lay with the defenders.

"Cover," Paco yelled as the woods around him came alive with bullets. Two men were instantly hit and went down screaming. They were pulled out of the line of fire, one dead and one seriously wounded. His men immediately returned fire. Automatic weapons fire tore into the top of the ridge. Paco nodded to the two men who carried the light anti-tank missiles. Between them they had ordinance for several shots.

"Shit," Paco yelled. There's more than one man up there," He yelled into his headset, "Echo one, you hear that?"

"Well boss, I guess we've got more than one man," Philippe yelled back.

"I hear a fifty," Paco said unbelieving.

"A fifty Cal?"

"Gotta be," Paco screamed back over the din. Then it all came to him. No intel on the family or friends.

"Keep cover and advance. Let's see how the fifty likes RPG rounds. Fire at will," Paco ordered.

To Nathan and Crockett it sounded like the whole woods came alive with gunfire and then the whoosh of an RPG and a huge explosion off to the side of the ridge.

"They're hot," John yelled, and Sam let loose with an RPG from the ridge.

For the next ten minutes it was absolute bedlam as each side peppered the other with automatic gunfire. Twice an RPG had exploded within a few feet of the front of the trench. There was smoke and dirt everywhere, across the ridge and down the slope to where the three advancing units took cover and moved up the ridge. Sam was bleeding from several places. The helmet and body armor that he had insisted his father and the other men wear had easily saved each of them from serious harm or death. Shrapnel flew in all directions as the ground shook. Neither side could keep this pace up for long. John had stowed plenty of ordinance but not for a damn siege. He knew the enemy would have limited time to carry out their mission. Even though Patience was isolated, the sound of a full scale battle would attract attention and outside law enforcement would arrive. He both welcomed and feared that happening. If their attackers were trapped, they would try to fight their way out. Modern law enforcement is well armed, but these were well trained mercenary soldiers. John's intention was to defend and to send a message. If the enemy intended to take the ridge, many of them would die doing so.

It was during this initial madness that Nathan took up his spears and the huge shotgun slung over his shoulder and began to run, crashing through the woods all along the perimeter of the ridge and behind the attackers. The first man he took had no time to react. As he fired his RPG, Nathan threw a spear through him with such force that it was embedded in a tree several feet beyond. The man's entire head was just gone. The man had been hit with a spear easily weighing thirty pounds. It tore through him like a freight train going through a watermelon, without slowing at all. The shaft of the spear was tipped with a blade several inches wide and an inch thick. Only a dark flash was seen by the other men as Nathan crashed through, firing both barrels of a .8 gauge shotgun, spraying buckshot into more than one man. The men had body armor but their legs, arms, and heads were exposed and were savaged by the buck shot. The enemy fired wildly back as Nathan charged by, but had little time for accuracy, pinned down by the defenders in front.

Nathan continued his attack, killing three men, tearing each apart with a massive spear. He targeted the men with the weapons that could do the most damage to his friends. The psychological effect on the attackers was pronounced. Even the combat hardened officers had never seen anything like it.

"Find me that man, Philippe. Take him out," Paco tersely ordered. He could not afford to be boxed in from the rear. He would eliminate the threat and then they would advance under an all-out barrage and deliver a satchel charge that would completely take out the entrenched position. Because of the angle of the hill, the rockets they fired struck dirt or impacted trees on their way to their target. He and his men were pinned down in prede-termined fields of fire, and that heavy caliber machine gun up there was pre-sighted on their position. He knew that the sheriff was Special Forces, but he sensed another hand in this. He was confronting an enemy trained in the type of warfare that he was, older, more traditional.

"Roger that." Philippe didn't have to ask who his commander meant. He spoke quick words to his next in command and slid off into the woods to find his man. Philippe too could move like a ghost in the woods, jungle, or any terrain for that matter. He would track the man.

Philippe soon caught a glimpse of a huge shape crashing through the undergrowth about seventy five yards behind and to the right of him. He smiled and thought "I have you now, my spear throwing friend." Guy must be nuts. A silenced weapon got the job done just fine, even a bow, but a spear? What the damn hell? The guy also had a shotgun, and that meant limited range. The man would have to stop at some point, and when he does, I've got him.

Nathan slowed after he'd put some distance between himself and the rear of the attackers. He kept to the densest part of the undergrowth and tried to remain as inconspicuous as possible. Even though he was in good shape, his heart pounded in his chest and he was gulping huge breaths of air. He needed to stop, take cover and assess his situation. He had never been in combat, but had trained for it all his life. He was proud not to feel fear; something else had taken over, something handed down from some of the fiercest warriors the world had ever known. As his breathing slowed he watched the woods in front of him and to the sides, missing the small shape dart far to the right and behind him.

Philippe came at Nathan's position from the behind and slightly to the side. He couldn't get a shot, as the man had positioned himself up against a huge tree covering his back. The little Philippe could see of the man was huge. He could also see the end of a side by side shotgun. Judging by the damage it had done it was a blunderbuss, had to be an eight gauge. He did not want that thing going off in his face. He didn't have a world of time either, and needed to get back to the line and take that hill and get the hell away from this crazy place. They had expected some possible resistance, but this was the most intense combat Philippe had ever seen. You couldn't even exaggerate it. Using the cover of the gunfight that continued, he used every skill in his arsenal to advance on the man. It would have to be quick and he held a side arm ready to fire as he crawled forward. His target shifted and he froze, all the while keeping the protruding barrel of the shotgun in sight. If it moved, he froze as he inched closer. He had been trained by the best the former Soviet Union provided. He had him either way. If the man broke cover he was dead. If he didn't move he was dead. He was less than five yards from the man now and had reached a point where it would be impossible for the man to bring that shotgun to bear in time. He just wouldn't be able to swing it around before he was shot. He readied and sprang, firing. It was too late by the time he saw the shotgun resting in the fork of a branch shoved into the ground. No! Phillipe screamed in his mind as he saw Nathan's giant hand dart out and grab his head with crushing power. As he tried to recover, he fired wildly off balance and was jerked off the ground and swung towards the massive trunk. Philippe's head smashed like a pumpkin against the side of the tree. Once was all it took. The force was so great that a dead limb fell along with some other forest litter.

Nathan tossed the man aside, grabbed his shotgun, and was gone. As he ran back towards the fighting, Nathan knew he'd gotten lucky. It hadn't been sound or sight that had given the man away. At the last minute Nathan smelled him. Away from the fighting the air was clear of smoke and gunpowder. Nathan knew what everything in those woods smelled like, and the whiff that caught his attention was not from that neighborhood. The man's smells were a product of what he ate and drank, what soaked out of his body and into his clothes during combat. The man was a casualty of exactly what Nathan used as his best defense, his knowledge. He was focusing all of his senses as he had been taught. John had known that if things got to the point where the ridge was under attack, Nathan would follow orders and come in from the rear, and further, that any decent commander on the ground would have to send someone back to neutralize that threat. Once again John had expected that their secret weapon was that they would be underestimated at all levels and then, once engaged, the enemy wouldn't realize their mistake until it was too late.

Nathan started to move back towards the battle when he heard someone running towards him from behind. The person was small, but never-the- less Nathan crouched and hid until he saw Jimmy Dent running at full speed towards him.

"Nathan, Nathan!!" The boy ran into Nathan full speed and grabbed onto him the best he could.

"Whoa, there, Jim! This is about the worst place you could be right now! Get out of here!"

"I heard guns, people shooting. What's wrong?" The boy was clearly near panic but Nathan could see he was holding it together. Nathan was nearly as worried as the kid. The men on the ridge were trapped and in trouble.

"Jim, run to my house and call the airport. The number is on the wall by the phone. Tell Cecil that John Trunce is in trouble. He will know what to do".

"What if I don't get an answer?"

"Then drive my tractor out there and get him!"

"You be careful Nathan!"

"Yes sir, Jim. Now run as fast as you can!"

Nathan watched the kid tear off through the woods. He had a strange feeling inside. He really liked that kid. If they all made it through this he intended to introduce Jimmy to Sam and John. They'd love to meet any kid who sprinted towards a battle to find his friend. For now at least the kid would be safe. If he didn't get Cecil on the phone, it would take him an hour to drive out there on the tractor and this thing would be long over in an hour.

"Colonel, we're down to one RPG round. Plenty of grenades though," Joseph yelled out as he crouched down and reloaded.

"I don't know about you Joseph, but I never could throw worth a shit," John said.

As he spoke he looked over at Sam. He was everywhere. He moved with instinct and grace, if that was the word. He had never seen his son in combat, and prayed that he never would again. He was a sight to behold, a man in his prime. A soldier trained to the highest modern level, fighting with a magnificent ferocity. He'd seen a few men like that over the years, but not many. He would tell him that if they made it through this afternoon.

THIRTY-FIVE

Napping on a day bed in the back of the hangar, Cecil languished in the little cool of an air conditioner he had jammed into the window. The room was roughed off and finished with plywood paneling with all the creature comforts he needed, an old TV set, a fridge and a garbage can for his takeout pizza box. He'd taken more and more to hanging out in the hanger and keeping things in order at the airport. His wife had passed away, and he didn't like bouncing around in the big old house with people stopping by to see if he was okay. It just wasn't in his nature to be rude. Manners were manners. So he just preferred to hide out. He had lots of money, both from his work and from his wife's large inheritance. Everyone always wanted some. The comments he'd get from so-called friends about it drove him nuts. The people he'd have gladly given huge amounts to, like his fly buddy John, didn't seem to care about it one way or the other. He glanced at the cell phone John had given him, and it seemed to be working. Honestly, he really couldn't tell. He knew there was a possibility these drug dealers might try to cause some trouble, but John had figured the likelihood of anything happening that couldn't be handled quickly was remote. He figured John would get word to him if necessary.

Miles out of town, Cecil couldn't hear the gunfire or the explosions, especially since he was practically underneath the air conditioner with the game turned up on the television. All at once his solitude was broken by the peal of the old rotary phone that shrilled on the metal desk. The one he had been thinking about opening the bottom drawer on. The one with the Old Crow bottle filled with the big man's moonshine, as he liked to call it. John and he shared some now and then, and joked that if they ever got tired of drinking it they could always put it in the Thunderbolt. He snatched up the phone and there was a kid on the other end jabbering excitedly. He caught Mr. Trunce, Nathan and fight. Then in the midst of all the chatter, he clearly heard, "Nathan says Sam and John are in trouble, trapped up on the ridge behind the farm." The phone dropped from his hand and crashed onto the desk as he scrambled for the plane. Cecil reacted like he had with the RAF during the Battle of Britain. He had been among a small group of American pilots who had volunteered for combat duty.

He was almost as much British as American. He had been born in the United States, to an American father and a British mother. As a child he spent many summers in the English countryside with his grandparents. When Germany attacked by air, Cecil was not willing to wait until the US entered the war. He enlisted in the RAF without hesitation. He and his fellow pilots won that battle at enormous expense. Although he flew many missions as the war continued nothing compared to those days backed against the wall living in a limbo between life and death. Twice he had his plane shot out from under him, only to find himself in another cockpit just hours later. He flew two flags in his yard, the stars and stripes and the Union Jack.

Cecil climbed up the ladder, hit the switches, and fired the engine. It caught immediately as the 2450 horsepower Pratt & Whitney engine roared to life. A few modifications had been made to the plane, and it leapt down the runway in response to his hand on the stick. Cecil checked his instrumentation as he picked up speed. He didn't have to warm this monster up, it wanted to go. Earlier in the day he'd checked and rechecked everything on the flight checklist along with the eight 50 caliber machine guns and the ten five inch rockets.

Within a few short minutes, he was in the sky and banking towards town. He realized that he had no radio contact and would have to make his decisions on his own. John and he had clear discussions about what action to take. If he was called into battle, it was all or nothing, and that's where things seemed to stand right now.

By the time the people of Patience took notice of the gunfire and explosions they heard in the distance coming from the Trunce farm, they also heard the Thunderbolt tearing across the sky at 400 miles per hour. Everyone looked up and wondered what that wild man was doing now. Hearing gun fire and explosions wasn't necessarily that out of place over there, but this seemed like the whole woods were coming alive.

John, Sam, Joseph and TJ were firing in all directions. There wasn't time to think of escape, they'd fired their last RPG and used up all of the grenades. The top of the ridge was covered with smoke and the air was like the inside of a bee hive: complete chaos. Just as John was switching ammo and deciding to at least try and get the other men out, he heard a sound like the sweet music of heaven and started to chuckle and then to laugh uproariously. The others glanced over and were slower on the up take. John had flown that old plane a hundred times, and he knew her distinctive sound.

"That's Cecil, now you are going to see some shit!" he yelled. "Get ready to get down and I mean under the dirt!"

Just then a rocket exploded just behind the trench scattering the men and filling the air with debris. TJ had taken the worst of it and was out, Sam kept firing down the hill as he crouched.

Cecil assessed the situation at the top of the ridge instantly. Old memories and training flowed into his mind and hands as he turned viciously into a hard left dive and came plummeting towards the middle of the hill leading up to the trench. He had complete confidence in his plane and his abilities, and this time the thought of personal safety didn't even register, one last run, you sorry bastards, he thought. The plane plummeted with a terrifying roar, crushing down from above.

"De na fuck with thunder," he yelled in an exaggerated Scottish brogue and sent every rocket into the hill side and opened up with the 50 cals. It was like the whole world came down from the sky for the men on the ground. The rockets' explosive charge was beyond ridiculous. Meteors might as well have been hitting the earth. As soon as the Thunderbolt had been there, it was gone.

Cecil looked down as he winged over and shot up into the sky. "Holy shit, holy shit, holy shit," he simultaneously laughed and yelled.

"That ought to do it!" he said with measured finality. He leveled off around ten thousand feet and flew a tight pattern around the area. He knew that if routed, the enemy would likely try to escape by air. With helicopters now, people could get picked up in a hurry. His mind turned to air combat as he adjusted the buckle on his parachute and checked his ammo.

It was when he heard the Thunderbolt that Paco realized that this battle was over. There simply wasn't enough time to do anything other than yell to take cover. With the sound of battle, the plane was on them before there was time. Bodies flew everywhere. The remaining rockets exploded as the area lit up in a massive flash and explosion. The concussion pounded the men into the ground. The plane's rockets hit in twos ripping into the base and slopes of the ridge.

When Paco raised his head, only a handful of the men were alive. He was in complete shock. He had the presence of mind to call for a retreat and made contact with the jet. Who are these people? They had been dive bombed by a vintage combat aircraft. The men that could still walk were carrying the wounded. Less than half of his men survived. Thankfully, the firing from the top of the hill had stopped. As he turned to scramble away he caught a silhouette on top of the ridge. He knew he'd seen it before. It felt like someone had stepped on his grave. He immediately recognized the worn khaki jacket with an airborne insignia. The man looked old and grizzled. At least we had our asses handed to us by soldiers, he thought. This battle had been lost and he needed to get his wounded and remaining troops out alive. He cursed the fact that there would be no time to carry out their dead, he had to take care of the living.

The pilot in the Lear immediately responded to Paco's call and prepared to land the plane on the highway, as previously arranged in the event that extraction was necessary. He scanned the sky for the phantom combat aircraft Paco had hurriedly told him about. He kept his composure but lacked any combat experience. He'd spent most of his time in the air smuggling drugs. I'm a sitting duck, he thought, I just hope I can outrun whatever is out there. He couldn't hear anything over the din of the Lear's jet engines. As he approached the highway to land he did a quick fly by to make sure there were no vehicles on the road. He didn't want to be on the ground long. As he flew by he could still see thick smoke rising from the woods along the edge of the highway. What in the hell had happened? This was not good. Finally he could see the men on the ground, and they looked like they'd been chewed up and spit out.

As soon as the plane hit the ground, Paco and his men scrambled onto the aircraft. Philippe was gone and Manolo didn't look like he'd make it anywhere. All of the men had a wild look of complete disbelief. They were covered in dirt, sweat and blood. Several were singed by the explosive power of the rockets. The smell of burnt flesh permeated the cabin. The pilot slammed the door behind him, not bothering to ask if there were any stragglers. He engaged the engines and raced down the highway, launching into the sky as soon as he had sufficient speed. He shot towards the clouds to put as much distance as possible between the plane and whatever was on the ground.

Cecil watched the Lear land and take off seconds later. Once again he was left with a decision to make. He had no idea if the Lear had any weapons, or if others were about. He immediately dropped out of a cloud bank and engaged the Lear, coming out of the sun into the other pilot's blind spot. He exhausted his remaining 50 caliber rounds and watched as the bullets tore into the wings and engines of the aircraft. The effect was immediate. The Lear continued to try to gain altitude but couldn't, and the pilot was struggling to maintain any control at all. The plane hurtled to the east and out of Patience County.

Paco watched as the interior of the plane filled with smoke and when the electrical fires started, he knew they would crash. Men were yelling as he watched the pilot fight the controls through the open door to the cockpit. He calmly put on his seat belt and gave one last order "Belt yourselves in!" he yelled. He had always wondered how he would finally meet his end. Shot down by a relic. Obviously God had a sense of irony. He looked out the window and saw the ground coming up fast. Whispering a silent prayer that some of the men would survive; he bent forward in his seat and covered his head.

Sheriff Baker sat on his deck and looked lovingly down at his dock on the river. The water meandered pleasantly past his grassy river front property. He had lucked out when this property had come up for sale ten years ago. He really hadn't been able to afford it, but it was such a good deal and such a great spot, he just had to make it work. He could deal with the hassles of the crazies, the druggies, and the downright stupid as long as he could fish the river on the weekends and sit on this deck and have a cocktail in the evenings. There was always something going on when you lived on water, especially when it was a river with traffic. He had just saved up for the down payment on a new bass boat, and there it was, all shiny and new. He got everything on it. Hell, half of the fun was figuring out all of the things the bells and whistles and extra gadgets did. He loved his wife, but the boat was a great way to visit his buddies on the river, by himself. He had just sat down from freshening his Jack Daniels when he heard the sound of a jet engine getting louder and louder. Some dumb ass flying too low? What the damn hell? He didn't even have time to leap to his feet as he watched a small jet slam into the side of his beloved new boat and explode with a deafening roar. His house was set way back from the river on a hill to avoid flooding, but it shook all the same when the fuel exploded. He felt the wave of heat hit him like a straight line wind. He managed to hold onto his drink as the blast subsided and a cloud of black smoke rose into the air. He didn't get up. He reached for his cell phone and dialed two numbers, first the Fire Department and then his office. As he walked down towards the crash site he could see what little was left of the jet settling into the water, hissing and smoking. His boat was just gone. Little pieces of carpet hung in a tree down by the beach. He drained his drink and set his glass down on the river bank. Carefully, he took out his wallet and pulled out his badge and in an exaggerated motion skipped it out into the river.

"That's it for me," he muttered, and turned back up the hill.

"Jesus, Sheriff, you okay?" the fire chief said as he ran up. "What happened?"

"Air Trunce landed, and don't bother calling the FAA. They won't be coming. Damn cowboys," he said, looking off in the direction of Patience County.

THIRTY - SIX

"Cuban regulars is my guess," Joseph said leaning over a boot print as the men walked around the area where their attackers had been before Cecil's attack. There were shell casings scattered around the craters carved out by the rockets. Sam picked up a rifle that had been hastily cast aside when their attackers retreated.

"Cubans?" Sam said. "How do you know?"

"I've seen enough Russian issue boot tracks to last a lifetime," Joseph said.

"That, the weapons they were using, and this," John said as he held up a cigar butt.

"Hope the guy enjoyed it," Sam said. "If I'm not mistaken, I heard a jet land and some more firing."

"I'm quite sure Cecil put a few rounds into him," John said.

"Man, I hope like hell that we don't have a crashed plane in somebody's back yard," Sam said, relieved beyond belief that everyone was alive. "That definitely got a tad wilder than I would have thought."

"They certainly underestimated the situation. My guess is that they would have hightailed it south," Joseph added. "Lots of nothing but woods that way."

"Time to get moving back to town. I'm worried about the rest of the crew. It stands to reason that they might have sent men after our families," Sam said as he walked towards John's jeep.

"Not a scratch on her," John said and smiled, just as Nathan came jogging up.

Sam jumped out and went over to Nathan where they quite unashamedly grabbed each other by the arms.

"I left a few in the woods back there," Nathan said gesturing over his shoulder.

"Nathan, another great victory for the Masai!" John yelled.

"And the Airborne," Nathan said in deference to his father and John.

"Don't forget Special Forces," TJ said nodding at Sam.

"Nor the US Army Air Corps," John said pointing to the sky. "Saved my ass again."

"Let's regroup at Madeleine's," Sam said.

"I better go talk to Cecil. We might have to hide that plane," John said earnestly.

"I'll call Moon and ask him to make the call to Tracy," Joseph said. "We'll cover those bodies for burial later."

"This time Tracy's going to want a 'no more shit promise,' Sam," John said.

"I hope this will be the last time," Sam said with little certainty.

"Can't have Mexican meth gangs in Patience though," John said.

"We'll talk to Tracy and see what he can do to put this thing to bed," Sam added. "The good people of Patience aren't going to turn a blind eye to full-scale warfare in their back yards. Next time I'm taking my fight to them. Let's see how they like assassins and soldiers in their back yards!"

John took in the scene and knew this had been his last battle and it had been a victory. Without doubt soldiers fought on both sides. If the remainder of the war had to be taken to the enemy, that would be for Sam and Tracy. His last command had been to save his son, and he was thankful that he had prepared Sam as well as he had for life and battle. Their victory was magnificent, but in the future it was Sam the men needed to look to for leadership.

As the men drove into the yard at the restaurant they saw the delivery van, and could sense from the air of the place that something serious had happened. They jumped from their vehicles and ran into the restaurant. Madeleine, Karen, Christine, and Yves were calmly sitting around the family table off in the corner by the window next to the kitchen, eating and sipping wine. Sam was the first to the table and put his arms around Christine and Yves and hugged them close. Sam was covered in dirt and was bleeding from several superficial cuts and a couple of pretty good gouges, but it was clear nobody was worried about getting dirty. The others looked at Sam, Christine, and Yves and the strengthening of a new branch of their family. Christine and Sam were locked in a kiss in the middle of everyone with Yves arms around them.

John walked up and embraced everyone.

"Oh John, I was so worried, it sounded like World War Three back there. Is everybody okay?" Karen said.

"Just fine. Hell of a fight, as crazy as I've ever seen. I just want to tell you I had soldiers with me!"

"You should have seen Madeleine, John, I was only afraid for you," Karen said, burying her face in her husband's dirty jacket.

"Merci Madeleine," John said without asking what had happened. He knew that he would find out in due time.

"It was nothing. I just had to get a couple of pigs out of my restaurant," she said airily, with a wave of her hand.

"Anything we might need to do yet to follow up?" Sam said.

"When I open tomorrow it would be nice to have the delivery truck moved," Madeleine, said as if they were discussing moving tables around for a larger party.

"I think we can move it now," Sam said.

Nathan came into the room and the hugging started all over again.

"Are we done playing army Sammy? Because I have got better things to do than have people coming after me in the woods, airplane attacks, and in general wondering who the hell is going to be shooting next."

Sam glanced out the window at that point and noticed a darkened SUV creep by. He noticed the driver peek into the restaurant and continue down the road.

"No way, he muttered, there's the dumb ass now," Sam murmured.

Sam ran from the building and jumped into the delivery van. Sure enough, keys in the ignition. He fired up the ungainly vehicle and slammed it into gear and drove after the SUV. He glanced over his shoulder as the three dead bodies rolled around behind him. There's always the car crusher over at the scrap yard, he thought.

Jose looked into the rear view mirror and saw the delivery van hurtling towards him. Once he got over the shock of seeing that crazy sheriff in his rear view mirror, he floored the accelerator and the vehicle shot forward.

"Why can't people cooperate with my plans and just die!" Jose said to Lion, who at this point was jumping from the front to back seat with great glee at the new game. He could sense the excitement in the air, and wanted to be part of the action.

"What kind of a dumb ass brings a dog on a military operation, especially a coon hound?" Sam muttered, catching a glimpse of the animal. Having grown up in rural Missouri, he knew just the extent of the 'usefulness' of man's best friend, which was to hunt coon, period. Sam floored the gas and knew he had one chance to stop this guy and he was going to take it. The SUV was pulling away, and Sam suddenly veered left and took a gravel road, lurching and bouncing wildly. The boxes in the van crashed off the shelves on top of the bodies. It took everything he had to stay on the road. He flew past a dead end sign, never taking his foot off the accelerator.

Jose looked back in the rear view mirror and sped down the access ramp and onto the main highway and the hell out of town.

It's too bad there was nobody around to see what happened next. Even Jose didn't see it coming. Just as he got onto the highway the delivery van flew through the air and collided with the SUV, landing almost entirely on the front seat, mashing it down flat. The two vehicles careened wildly off the highway, down an embankment and into a swamp, coming to an abrupt, soupy stop. Sam finally stopped rocking back and forth and thanked everything and everybody that his seatbelt had held. He slid from the vehicle and surveyed the damage, surprised as hell that there was no fire. He massaged his shoulders where the belt had dug in and as he looked around he just shook his head, thinking, I shouldn't be alive. Sam didn't bother to look at the driver. It's hard to hide in a flat sardine can, he thought. He looked in the back seat and to his utter amazement there was a white dog, tongue out, wagging his tail, seemingly just waiting for somebody to open the door. It took a little effort, but Sam got it open enough for the dog to slide out and hop up on his chest and lick his face.

"Some dogs just pick the wrong masters, isn't that right boy," he said as he fluffed the dog's ears.

"I know lots of coon hunters who'd love to meet you, a good ole Treeing Walker! Yep, lots of coons in Patience, no crime though, boy."

Carlos waited until it was dark and then left the state park where he had been staying in the modest camper. Following Manny's orders, he'd stayed away from the action in case there was bad news to report. He left payment in a yellow envelope and dropped the pieces of his cell phone into the garbage can on the edge of the park. He thought back over the course of the day. He'd tried to raise that idiot Jose on the phone once he heard the battle begin. He knew better than to get involved in that, and had waited until things had settled down to go out and reconnoiter. He drove a smaller, street legal motorcycle around and surveyed the damage. Once he'd seen Jose's car pancaked by their delivery van down in the swamp, he knew he'd have to find another employer. He also needed some way to tell Manny the Farmer what had happened. Although he was sure Manny would tell him to come home, Manny was a bad ass after all, and he didn't want to end up as fertilizer in the agaves field. Time to reassess his options. Option one, run like hell, grab his stash of cash and sell hats on the beach somewhere and never appear on the radar screen again. Without further thought he headed towards the airport in St. Louis, a safe deposit box, and a one way ticket to South America.

CHAPTER
THIRTY-
SEVEN

Manny sat at a pleasant seaside table in a nondescript little bar down by the beach in Havana. He absently twirled his drink and sighed as a cool breeze blew in off the water. He had left all of his concerns behind him. He hadn't heard anything from Carlos or Jose, but his concern with that matter was waning. He assumed it had gone according to plan. . He sipped his tequila, pleased to see his own brand on the shelf in this quaint and sleepy little place. He shifted in his seat and gazed out at the sunset, absolutely magnificent. There's nothing like a Caribbean evening. Abruptly a shadow passed over his closed eyes, sat down and spoke in a low, commanding tone.

"Please don't bother to get up Manny, your man is sleeping under the palm tree over there," Tracy said, pointing to a man stretched out on a hammock with a hat over his face.

"To whom am I speaking?" Manny said without great fear. He had sized up the situation quickly. If the man had wanted him dead he would be dead, a poisoned drink, or something nasty shoved in his ear.

"I don't exist, but your friends in Washington send their regards."

"I see. Do my friends have any message of importance for me?"

"They have very important interests in a small county in Missouri called Patience, and there were some problems there recently."

"I see. And how can I, a humble Agaves farmer, be of service?"

"Even though I recognize your modesty, you are known to be a resourceful and influential man. Perhaps you could spread the word to any of your countrymen or other businessmen who you might be acquainted with, and suggest to them they should ply their trade elsewhere."

Manny looked at the man, and kept trying to see into the depths of his eyes, nothing, flat like a dark and bottomless lake. The fine scars on his faced looked like they had been inflicted by a professional. Those that survived interrogations of that nature were hard men indeed. He had dealt with few like this man before. He looked, spoke, and felt like everything the conspiracy theorists talk about. He wondered in passing if this guy slept in his native soil at night, in a castle in a faraway land.

"I have been out of touch with my friends in Washington, how is it they found me?"

"Why, your Uncle Fidel, of course. He worries about you too, or so it would seem. So Manny, what are your plans for the future?"

"I believe I will retire and remain in Cuba, maybe a little travel?" Manny said in a questioning tone.

"And your friend's request?"

"My friends need not worry."

"With that understanding I will say farewell, Manny, our business is concluded. As I leave, shall I order you a freshener?" Tracy said as he gestured towards the empty glass in Manny's hand.

"Yes please, ask them to bring the bottle if you would."

"Of course, sir."

Manny sat more than a little shaken. Now that was a bona fide spook. He waited until the waiter came to the table with the bottle and a small plate of pickled fish, before he slowly turned around. He really didn't expect to see the man any longer, nor did he ever want to see him again.

As he sat, he decided that this whole thing was done. Regardless of what had happened it was over. He had lots of money and had provided for the families of his workers, with an employee owned co-op. "Good luck, my friends," he said as he bit into a piece of the fish and washed it down with a healthy swallow of tequila.

CHAPTER
THIRTY-EIGHT

Doc and Bucket stood on the sidewalk outside the Chicago Bus depot. Twice in less than ten minutes, they'd been propositioned to buy dope. Doc was ready to leave and having heard nothing out of Patience, he knew that things could not have gone well. There had been some scuttlebutt from some of his connections about more rocket propelled grenades and giant black guys. Technically, without further orders his job was done. The meth he made had just been unloaded at bargain basement prices to a guy he knew, in the men's room. Since his employer wasn't out any real money, as the cost to make the stuff was minimal, so there wouldn't be any huge tears or people looking for him because they were out any big money. Now it was time to ship the kid.

"Well, it's time to break camp buddy, here," he tucked a couple of hundreds into the kid's pocket along with a small amount of meth. He didn't want any withdrawal issues with the kid until he was far away from this happy place.

"What's up Doc?" the kid laughed, his big maw opening and closing.

"You get on that bus there and give them this ticket," Doc said, sliding a ticket into the kid's hand.

"Where you going?" Billy said.

"Have to go to Australia, been ordered. Well, have a nice trip." Doc walked the kid over to the bus and pushed him up the stairs and waited for the door to close and the bus to pull out. Then he walked briskly to his own bus headed to Northern California, where he could grow dope in peace. Enough of this shit. No more nosy neighbors, no more bucket jawed dummies, and no more Mexican Mafia. He sat down on the bus next to some grungy-assed kid.

"Hey man, got any weed?" the kid just had to ask.

Doc rolled his eyes and said, "Now none of that kid, I'm a cop."

"Oh shit, man, only kidding," the kid blurted out.

"I'll make you a deal. You don't speak at all until you get off the bus and I won't hassle you about it, okay?"

"Yah man, whatever you say."

"You're talking there, son."

The kid nodded and made a zipping motion in front of his mouth. Is it me? Doc thought as he revised his plan to live way up in the mountains.

Sam and Nathan sat next to each other on the gravel sand bar on the edge of their swimming hole and relaxed in the sun. They had a line down into the creek to catch whatever or nothing at all. Christine lay on a yellow foam mat, soaking up the sun in a tiny bikini bottom and no top, golden and perfectly proportioned. Although sprawled in a careless way, it didn't hurt her looks any.

"Most of the time she's nearly naked, Sammy," Nathan spoke under his breath.

"I know you're not complaining," Sam laughed.

"Just for my information, how do you get a woman who looks like that to do that?"

"Import them from Southern France."

"Gotta love the French," Nathan sighed.

"I do."

Cecil and John stood next to the Thunderbolt, tucked carefully back and out of sight in a private hangar.

"Damn good flying, Cecil. You flat saved our ass," John said, clapping him on the back.

"I gotta tell you John, I haven't felt this good since before the wife passed away."

"Apparently you just need some stimulating activity, Cecil, although a little less stimulating or we'll spend our golden years breaking rocks somewhere."

"Anything on the crashed plane?" Cecil asked.

"Damn commuter accident. Those things just can't seem to stay in the air," John said with a wry smile.

"They just don't make them like they used to."

"Only brave pilots, Cecil, only brave pilots."

"You have to keep an eye on them, Moon, no more exploding commuter vehicles, rockets, or crashed commercial aircraft. It's not good for tourism," Tracy said, not entirely joking.

"Can we expect any other visits Tracy?" Moon spoke into the scrambled phone.

"After Trunce's grey army defeated the bad guys, it'll be a damn legend. Nobody's coming down the pike. I've got a constant bead on the applicable traffic now. Besides that, there's no crime in Patience to speak of."

"Where? Who?" Moon mimicked, both men laughing as they hung up.

Madeleine walked through the dining area and watched her friends and neighbors eating their evening meal. She loved the hum and feel of the restaurant but now it was Christine's turn. Christine and Yves could live upstairs until Sam made an honest woman out of her. Things would have to wait until that bastard of a husband of Christine's signed the divorce paperwork. He would sign the papers soon, Madeleine thought. It's just a matter of me explaining things to him. She smiled as she thought of her flight the next day to Marseilles. Better her than Sam to speak to the man. Men just don't understand these things, she thought.

ACKNOWLEDGEMENTS

The author would like to thank his friends, parents and family for their assistance, contributions and steadfast support for *The Patience County War.* I would like to thank my primary editor, Annie Chase for her invaluable assistance. Special mention goes to LuAnne Borders and Ben Oney for their editorial assistance as well.

Fic
PETR

1118855

19.95

MN Author

Made in the USA
Charleston, SC
28 December 2011